Raven Spirit

by

Pam Binder

The Haunting of Pinedale High Series

Copyright Notice
This is a work of fiction. Names, characters, places, and incidents are either the product of the author's imagination or are used fictitiously, and any resemblance to actual persons living or dead, business establishments, events, or locales, is entirely coincidental.

Raven Spirit

COPYRIGHT © 2024 by Pamela Binder

All rights reserved. No part of this book may be used or reproduced in any manner whatsoever without written permission of the author or The Wild Rose Press, Inc. except in the case of brief quotations embodied in critical articles or reviews.
Contact Information: info@thewildrosepress.com

Cover Art by *Lea Schizas*

The Wild Rose Press, Inc.
PO Box 708
Adams Basin, NY 14410-0708
Visit us at www.thewildrosepress.com

Publishing History
First Edition, 2024
Trade Paperback ISBN 978-1-5092-5882-6
Digital ISBN 978-1-5092-5883-3

The Haunting of Pinedale High Series
Published in the United States of America

Dedication

To my grandsons, Jimmy and Jakey.
True warriors with hearts of gold.

Chapter One

Bathed in shadows beneath the clouds, the body of a high school student hung from the goalpost in the endzone of Pinedale High's football field. The young man's eyes were frozen open in an expression of fear and shock. A pair of ravens, with pitch black feathers that shone with a purple iridescent glow, circled above the victim, watching and waiting.

Spotting their target, they dipped their wings and flew toward the opposite end of the field by the school's bleachers. Another young man, tall, lean, with high cheekbones and almond-shaped eyes, prepared to begin his evening jog on the track that circled the football field like a coiled snake.

Nate Collier finished lacing his shoes, straightened to stretch, and noticed the ravens' approach. They settled on the bleachers nearest to him. "Edgar. Allan. It's just me tonight." They had appeared two years ago when he was a freshman. He'd been having lunch by himself on the bleachers, dreaming of making the varsity track team. He'd shared his lunch with them, and it had become a habit. He'd named them after his favorite writer.

The tallest of the two hopped over to him and cocked his head to the side.

"Sorry. I forgot to bring food. Other things on my mind. I'm thinking Aaron's a no-show."

He clenched his jaw against the reason his jogging

buddy might be late. A wave of regret hit him like a blow to the chest. He and Aaron had fought earlier in the day. What did it say about him that he was more comfortable around animals than people? Nothing good.

Nate buried the emotion alongside a growing list and took off on a slow jog to warm up. He preferred taking the trail in the forest on the perimeter of the school's grounds, but the path around Raven Lake was pitch black at this time of year, not that it was that much better on the track. The sun had set, and the moon, and most of the stars, were hidden under a thin layer of clouds. The coaches must have forgotten to turn the lights on after football practice this afternoon.

But regardless, he didn't want to miss Aaron in case he did show up here. They'd fought over a girl—so maybe Aaron was still upset. Nate didn't blame him. Nate had been an idiot. But he hadn't been the only person on edge lately.

Nothing had been the same since the town of Pinedale had the bright idea that they needed to remodel the stadium. Construction started a year ago by tearing down bleachers and excavating the ground on the visitors' side. Work ground to a standstill when the remains of a mansion and bones were unearthed that dated back to colonial times. Construction had been ordered halted while the courts decided how to proceed.

No one talked about the accidents and ghost sightings.

Shadows deepened as Nate rounded the corner on the track, picking up speed as he headed in the direction of the endzone and the construction site. The same ravens he'd seen earlier dive-bombed him and croaked out a scream.

"Hey. Edgar. Allan. What'd I do to you? We talked about this. We're friends. Not cool."

He tripped over a dark pile of debris in the track and went down. Feathers and the bodies of dead ravens flew around him like a black cloud. He scrambled back to his feet. "What the…"

Edgar and Allan croaked out another scream and flew toward the endzone. A funnel of lights flickered, where moments before there had been only shadows. More ravens swept in from the east and darkened the night skies. The ravens were trying to warn him.

The hair on the back of his arms prickled like the time he was running on a trail at night and they'd warned him that the path ahead had been washed out by a storm. If he hadn't heeded their advice, he would have run off a cliff. There were names used to describe a group of ravens this size, and none of them were positive. They were called a conspiracy, an unkindness, or a rave.

Nate called them his friends.

Ravens were common in his town and so numerous that a tourist industry had grown up around them. Where most ignored the birds and kept their distance, Nate had befriended them. What he had learned was that it was never a good thing when so many showed up at the same time. Had they come because of the dead ravens? What had happened to them?

Ravens were predators and because of their size had few natural enemies, other than the occasional owl, eagle, or large hawk. But he had never heard of so many ravens being killed in a group the size he'd seen.

Even at this distance he sensed their collective gaze upon him. They were either trying to warn him or beckon him closer.

"This is a bad idea," he said under his breath. He should run in the opposite direction.

The chatter of the ravens increased as the cloud cover drifted overhead, exposing the glow of a half-moon that cast a pale yellow light over the endzone.

The light pulsated, illuminating the gaping excavation site that plunged three stories deep into an abyss. Shadows spread over the disturbed boulders and rocks like dark blood. A raven croaked out a scream and others joined him. Swinging from a rope attached to the goalpost's cross bar, the body of a young man swayed in an icy breeze.

The ravens stilled.

Nate trembled, clenching his hands into fists until his knuckles shone as white as bones. He forced his legs to step forward and acknowledge with his eyes what instinct tried to deny. He knew the young man.

The body turned slowly as though rotated by an invisible hand.

The face of the young man glowed pale white under the moon. Nate's breath caught and held. "No. No. No!" He dropped to his knees. "Aaron," he sobbed. "Who did this to you?"

Chapter Two

Above the football goalpost, where the body twisted in the autumn breeze and a young man tried desperately to cut the body down, an ashen-white funnel of light shimmered. It transformed into the image of a young woman with long hair and sad eyes and still dressed in the garments she had worn when she had been murdered—over four hundred years ago.

Fiona MacGregor hovered nearby, her cold heart aching for the loss of life, as she had done countless times before. She could not have done anything to prevent his death, or so her father had said when they witnessed the boy's attack. But she had stayed to make sure he crossed over and, if that failed, to stay and help him make the transition from a living to a ghost. It gave her purpose and a respite from her grief and her guilt.

They were dead, her father often said, when she pleaded with him to allow her to find a way to intervene. He told her she wasted her time. Why should either of them care if another living lost his life? No one had come to their aid. Besides, no one could see them, or hear them speak, and if they caught a glimpse, or heard a sound, it was to judge them monsters and run from them. It was the way of the world. And on and on her father's lecture had wound, as coiled and unforgiving as a poisonous snake.

But she did care. Had always cared. Yet she had

stood by for centuries, wishing she could do something, and in the end she had done nothing. She had been too weak and caught up in her own grief, not for her life, or even her father's, but for Jeremy's murder, the man she had loved and lost.

The young man succeeded in pulling the body down from the goalpost but was having difficulty untying the rope around his friend's neck. His eyes were swollen with tears, his voice begged and pleaded. "Why," he shouted over and over, each word softer and softer until the last word ended on a sob.

His deep voice, the way it filled with anguish, and his profile, with its prominent cheekbones, and hair that skimmed his wide shoulders, reminded her of Jeremy. She pressed her hand against her mouth to smother the sudden cry of pain.

It had been so long, but the grief and guilt were always just below the surface. She had tried to bury it, and sometimes hours passed when she had thought she had succeeded. Then the colors of a sunset, or the way the moon glistened over a mirror-smooth lake, would remind her of the stolen moments Jeremy and she had shared.

She gasped again, and whispered Jeremy's name aloud. The resemblance between Jeremy and the young man trying to revive his friend was uncanny. They looked so much alike they might have been twins.

The young man scrunched his eyebrows together and glanced in her direction. "Is someone there?"

Chapter Three

Heart pounding, Nate sat back on his haunches. He'd heard a woman's voice. Had there been a witness to Aaron's murder?

"Is someone out there? Don't be afraid. I just want to talk to you."

A man in a plain black ski mask tackled Nate and drove him to the rock-strewn ground, pinning him with his knee and shoving his hands down on Nate's shoulders. The man smelled of garlic, stale beer, and sweat, and he outweighed him by a good fifty pounds. Jagged rocks dug into his back. Nate struggled to twist free but felt as though he was pinned like a bug under glass.

Had the man surprised Aaron in the same way? His friend would not have stood a chance. The attack would have come as a surprise. Aaron wasn't a street fighter and took personal safety for granted. Aaron had been aware of Nate's struggles, but Nate wasn't sure if Aaron had internalized them much beyond that.

Aaron would have been alone and afraid. And instead of being there for his friend, Nate had been sulking, deliberately taking his time meeting Aaron. His friend's death was on his hands. Anger fueled his temper. The argument had been his fault.

Unlike Aaron, Nate was fully capable of fighting back.

Nate reared up and cracked his forehead against the man's head. Blood gushed from the man's wound, splattering over Nate. The man roared in pain, loosening his grip. Nate palmed a rock as he rolled to the side and stood. "That's for Aaron, you piece of shit. Get the hell away from me."

The man growled and dove for Nate again, wrapping his arms around Nate's waist to bring him down. He pressed a blade against Nate's neck, his eyes as black and cold as the water at Raven Lake. "Don't try that again. Hold still or I'll gut you like a fish."

Cold steel sliced into Nate's flesh. Warm blood soaked into his shirt. But it wasn't the first time he'd bled. Adrenaline surged through him. He used the rock he'd palmed and slammed it against the side of the man's face.

Startled, the man swore, loosened his grip on his knife, and swiped blood from his eyes. Nate seized his chance and punched the man again, then scrambled to his feet.

"Fred, what is going on here?" a man said, wearing a ski mask identical to that of the first man. He spoke with authority as though he was used to being in charge, but his voice sounded robotic as though he was talking through a device that could disguise a person's voice. "I leave you alone for a split second and all hell breaks loose." He pulled a handgun from under his black leather jacket and held it toward Nate. "Drop the rock, hot shot," he snarled. "Keep your hands up and your mouth shut."

Nate released the rock and raised his hands. He needed a distraction. If he could keep them talking, maybe someone would come along, or they would make a mistake. Not likely, but that's all he had.

More ravens glided from the night sky and joined the dozens perched on the goalpost's crossbar. They settled in position, folding their wings against their bodies silently as their eyes, as black as murder, trained on the tableau below. Their presence gave him courage. He was not alone.

"Let me go," he said with renewed purpose.

The man with the robotic voice chuckled. The tone echoed in the still night and seemed to awaken the ravens perched on the goalpost's crossbar. They squawked low as though in response. "You're hilarious, kid. We can't let you leave. You've seen too much."

"I won't say anything. You can trust me."

Fred turned to the man with the robotic-sounding voice. "What's happened to you? You told me we were just going to scare the boy. Why don't we do as this one says and get out of here? This place gives me the creeps. There have been ghost sightings since they dug up this place and found a bunch of old bones. Who knows what'll be crawling out next."

"I'm too close. No loose ends, and this kid is a loose end. He'll start asking questions like the other one. Hang the boy. We'll have to hang him, string the first one up again, if we're going to make this look like a double suicide."

Fred shuddered. "Are you out of your mind? I'm not touching a dead guy."

"Grow a pair. Like I said, we'll make it look like a double suicide. Might even make this one scribble a note. Anything else will draw suspicion. It's supposed to look like something a messed-up kid would do. Students at Pinedale High School are doing stupid things like this all the time. Do as you are told. We're getting paid to make this problem go away. Get the rope. And quiet those birds. They are getting on my nerves."

Chapter Four

The funnel of light in the endzone quivered. Fiona had tried to ignore the growing din of the ravens' screams. They were concerned for the young man and wanted her help. But she was a ghost, cursed to spend eternity in this form until she learned how to move on. Hadn't she done enough for the dead already? Recently, she'd learned her purpose was to help the newly dead adjust. But it was not an easy transition…for either them or her.

Fiona glanced toward the ravens. An icy breeze swept around them, stroking their feathers, as she focused on them, wondering why they had chosen the evening hour to gather. They usually roosted at night, preferring to hunt during the day. They represented many things to many people. Some thought of ravens as the harbingers of death, a genesis of rebirth, or messengers heralding change.

A few twisted their necks to gift her with a nod. Startled, she nodded in return. Amongst the most intelligent in the bird kingdom, they also possessed sharp eyesight, and she had made friends with them when she realized they sensed her presence. But again, why had they chosen this moment to gather? They knew she helped the dead. Was that the reason they remained? But their reactions were different tonight. They were intent on the young man below. Concerned for him. She sensed they did not want him to die.

She hovered closer, then held still. The young man reminded her so strongly of Jeremy, the man she had loved and lost. She shuddered again, fighting the urge to flee. As though sensing her confusion, one of the ravens screeched.

"Let me go," she whispered to them, using the same words the young man had said to his assailants moments before. But the ravens only squawked louder.

The men had the young man surrounded. But if she thought of it, she should not have been surprised at the ravens' presence. She had noted their strong attachment to the young man. The ravens were loyal creatures. She felt the all-too-familiar stab of guilt. It sliced through her like a steel blade. She should have gone with Jeremy when he first asked.

She ignored the heated words between the men in the black hooded masks, recognizing the moment the young man realized he might die. Instead of giving in to the inevitability of it and cursing the hand of an uncaring fate, his expression hardened.

Like her Jeremy, he was strong, resolute. But, also like her Jeremy, that would not save him.

Abruptly, the two men in masks jumped the young man, who fought to get free. Fiona knew it was useless. His assailants outweighed him and appeared much stronger. The one with the strange-sounding voice had a weapon. She had not been there to save the one the men had hung, but she could not stand by without trying to help the other. It was her experience in Scotland that even the most fearsome warriors were cautious and even afraid of ghosts, and she had learned that it was true here as well. But would it be enough? Her father would disapprove. Did she dare defy him?

She wavered. He cautioned that it was dangerous to connect with a living.

A raven cawed, and another joined. Like the game of dominoes, one after another added their voices, until the uproar blocked out all other sounds.

The men were so focused on securing a rope to the goalpost they did not appear to notice the clatter. They soon would.

She raised her arms and summoned the ravens to do her bidding. The sky darkened to a deep ebony black as scores of ravens took flight from the goalposts.

They flew toward the men in dark swirls and swoops like shadows in a storm-fed wind. They pecked and scratched. Blood beaded on the men's exposed skin while the birds tore and ripped their clothes.

The men's arms churned the air, attempting to drive the ravens away. They failed. Their efforts were futile. Both men screamed in pain and growing hysteria. The man called Fred hesitated for a moment, pointing toward Fiona as a new level of fear registered in his eyes.

His hand trembled. His eyes grew wide. "Ghost!"

She mouthed the word, "Boo."

Fred's eyes widened as a new level of terror took hold of him.

The two men raced toward the parking lot. The sky was so thick with ravens it looked as though the men were followed by a black cloud. The men's screams combined with those of the ravens and echoed through the night long after Fiona had lost sight of them.

The young man was safe.

Relief swept over her like a cleansing rain. With the help of the ravens, they had frightened away the men with masks. Her father was wrong. Helping the living had not endangered her. The men were afraid of her, not the other way around.

She basked in her newfound power. She had defied her father and survived. She turned her gaze toward the last place she had seen the young man. Instead of continuing to help his friend, or leaving as the men had, he gazed toward her unafraid.

"Who are you?" he said. "My name is Nate."

Chapter Five

Nate glanced in the direction of the men who had attacked him. They had disappeared in a trail of smoke and screeching tires. He raced toward Aaron, knowing the chances his friend was still alive were slim, but he had to try.

He checked for a pulse. There was none. Aaron's eyes were vacant and looked like they were covered with a milky lens. They stared straight ahead, with a puzzled expression. Nate swallowed down the lump in his throat and closed Aaron's eyes gently. None of this made any sense. Aaron didn't have an enemy in the world. Nate, on the other hand, had more than his fair share for the both of them.

Out of the corner of his eye he saw the same young woman he'd seen earlier. She was about his age and stood a short distance away in the shadows of the football bleachers. He had called out to her to thank you, but she had not responded. Was she afraid? No, he did not sense fear. She was the reason he was still alive. It was difficult to see her features clearly, but she had long hair and wore a dress that skimmed her ankles.

His hands trembled as he closed them into fists. His fear had turned to anger. "Thank you. They were trying to kill me. You saved my life, but how'd you do that with the ravens? It was as though you could communicate with them. All I can do is get them to not take my food."

A squirrel ran through her semitransparent leg, followed by a swirl of colorful autumn leaves. He stumbled back a few steps. "What just happened? You can't be." His voice went an octave lower. "You're a ghost?" He shook his head. "No, that's impossible. This is a nightmare." He paced around the end zone, avoiding the spot where his friend lay on the ground.

"Aaron's not dead," Nate continued. "This is all a sick dream. I'm having a nightmare. I'm seeing a ghost. My mother says I watch too many horror films. Any minute now my chemistry teacher is going to yell at me to wake up and finish taking my test."

She hated to have to tell him the truth; it would bring back the pain of losing his friend. But it could not be avoided. She spoke gently. "My name is Fiona. This is not a dream, but for your sake, I wish it were. I am so sorry. Your friend was murdered." She avoided admitting to the part that she and her father had stood by and not intervened when Aaron was killed.

His eyes brimmed with tears. For a moment she thought he would leave, but instead his shoulders slumped forward. He turned and walked slowly over to his friend and sank to his knees. He looked like he was holding his breath.

His voice was thick with emotion as he clenched and unclenched his fists. "Let me see if I understand what just happened. Those two men murdered Aaron. They tried to kill me, until a ghost appeared and ordered the ravens to attack them." He used the palm of his hand to wipe his eyes.

Fiona was impressed that he was so calm. Most in his position would have become hysterical. She nodded. "You are correct."

He sat back on his heels and stared unblinking at Aaron. "This sort of explains the strange stuff I've been seeing on the football field at night. It all started with the excavation. Last week, while Aaron and I were running the track, we thought we saw an old man with a sword trying to run us through with his blade. That guy looked crazed, but we never thought he was a ghost. He looked so real. So alive."

Fiona glided forward and reached out to comfort him, but he scrambled back. He held up a staying hand. "Stay where you are." He rubbed his hand over his eyes and for a moment looked much older than his seventeen or eighteen years. "You saved me. Why didn't you save Aaron?"

"I am not allowed to answer." That was a lie. She was becoming too much like her father. He had forbidden her contact with the living. But he did not heed his own advice. She wished with all her strength that she was no longer visible, and she began to fade into the cool breeze.

Nate stood and spun around in a wide circle. "Wait. I'm sorry. Don't leave. Where'd you go? I can't see you anymore."

Just as well, she thought.

As she turned to leave, she paused. She sensed men approaching again. They were different from the last. And these intruders did not care if they were overheard.

In the distance a siren shrieked. The football stadium's lights snapped on, turning the night into day. In a matter of minutes, the football field came alive as though it were a game day. Paramedics, EMTs, and police officers raced in Nate's direction.

"Put your hands over your head and step away from

the body," a voice boomed out over a megaphone.

Nate did as he was ordered. "Am I glad to see you," Nate said, talking fast as police officers approached. "Someone killed my friend and was planning on hanging me, but the craziest thing happened. There was this ghost and then ravens attacked and drove the killers away."

The officer with the gun holstered his weapon. "Slow down, son. How'd you get those injuries?"

"I told you. I was attacked, and the men tried to put a rope around my neck, but these ravens and a ghost…"

The other officer grinned. "Hey, Detective Morrison, I'd say that for once a tip paid off. We have our suspect and can close this case in record time. And, bonus, this guy gave the best alibi ever. Never heard of using ghosts and ravens as a get-out-of-jail-free card. Were these those prehistoric ravens," he said to Nate, "or just your ordinary, everyday, shiny-object-stealing ravens?"

"That's enough, Billings," Detective Morrison said, frowning. "Keep it professional and give the boy a break. The young man claims the victim was his friend. If this kid is innocent of the crime, he's in shock. If he's guilty, well, then we have our suspect and he'll have his day in court. What I'm most concerned about right now is his injuries. The burn marks around his neck are consistent with rope burns. We'll take him in for questioning and let the lawyers sort it out." To Nate, Morrison said, "You'll need to call your parents."

"It's just me and my mom."

Chapter Six

Fiona materialized behind the trees. Her father said a living could not see a ghost unless they willed it. But Nate had seen her. How was that possible? She could prove to the policemen that Nate was telling the truth. But as she stepped out of the shadows, her father appeared and placed a hand on her arm, holding her back.

The living are of no concern to us," he said.

She hesitated. The man Nate had described a short time ago as an old man who had attacked him and his friend with a sword could only have been her father. He usually liked to brag about those he scared away. He had forbidden her contact with the living yet did not heed his own advice. All the dark feelings she had kept buried threatened to overwhelm her. But she was wary of challenging her father.

"Nate is different. I can feel it. He is like those who can see us even if we do not wish to be seen. That means we should help him."

Her father glanced toward Nate, his face lost in the shadows. "Even if the lad has the gift of sight, those possessing it can be a danger to themselves and others. They do not fear us as others might. It is more reason not to interfere."

"We cannot leave him. Nate is innocent. He did not kill that young man."

"Do not question me!" Her father's voice thundered

so loud the police officers approaching Nate from the parking lot turned, looking around, no doubt believing a storm was approaching. "For all we know," her father's voice rumbled in anger as he continued, "the lad may have had something to do with the murder. Leave him to his fate. Remember the last time you tried to interfere?"

Fiona nodded reluctantly. Her heart ached with the memory of that fateful night so long ago, the night she lost everything.

Chapter Seven

The next morning at school, Nate parked his Jeep in the school's parking lot and rested his head on the steering wheel. Last night was a blur. He couldn't believe Aaron was gone. His mom had come from work at the town's movie theater to the precinct. She had been polite to the police until they suggested Nate might be a suspect in Aaron's murder. She turned into a wolf defending her cub and had used terms like "allegation," "*prima facie*," and "right to counsel." He had forgotten that his mom attended a year of law school before she got married.

The police backed down and Nate had not been charged. But they were quick to add that the investigation was still open. It had been the only bright spot in what had been a nightmare experience.

He leaned against the driver's seat, glancing toward the parking lot. Students were grouped into packs or herds, depending on whether they were predators or prey. Members of the cheer squad held court in the center of the parking lot in clear view of the football, basketball, and baseball stars who posed to have their pictures taken by adoring fans. The next circle contained members of the less popular sports like swimming, track and field, and wrestling. Next were the members of the band, followed by the chess club and the various science clubs.

On the extreme perimeter were those who

considered themselves rebels and walked to the sound of their own drumbeat. They dressed in bright colors, stripes, checks, or polka dots, and the more their clothes defied fashion the better. Or they dressed all in black, which was Nate's personal choice, as it made picking out stuff to wear easier. But even this group of students knew their place in the school's food chain.

This last group was where he fit in the best. It was comfortable, and in its own way safe and a way to connect with like minds.

The fall weather had turned bitter, and a flock of clouds swept across the morning sky, turning day into night. He hadn't been charged, but that didn't mean he was home free. He had learned to gauge facial expressions, calculating who were friends and who were foes, a survival tactic he'd learned at an early age.

Detective Morrison had treated him fairly and seemed to believe his story. Whether he did or not, just the fact that he had not laughed and called him delusional, or high on drugs, helped.

A man tucked in the shadows of the shade trees draped over the parking lot moved forward and knocked on Nate's window. He made a rolling motion with his hand, indicating that he wanted Nate to roll down his car window.

Nate complied, sitting up straighter as the man came into view. It was Hank, the school's janitor. He had worked at Pinedale High for years and Nate counted him as one of the good guys. "I'm heading into school."

Being a tall man, Hank knelt so he could face Nate eye to eye. "I am not worried about you making it to class on time. No one expected you be here today anyway, what with Aaron's death and all. I dropped by to see if you're okay."

"All good."

Hank lifted an eyebrow.

Nate leaned against the car seat again. "Okay. I feel like roadkill. That's the wrong expression, under the circumstances, but it fits."

Hank smirked, nodding slowly. "Actually, the expression fits well in this scenario. I have a strong visual." He paused. "Rumor has it that you saw a ghost."

"Ah." He chuckled, closing his eyes. "And ravens. Can't forget the ravens. They helped the ghost chase off Aaron's murderers. With a story like that, I'd be surprised if I'm not trending on social media."

"You are the man of the hour." Hank laughed. "No doubt about it."

"Is anyone talking about who could have murdered Aaron?" Nate's voice sounded raw in his ears. He swallowed down the stinging ache in his throat. He couldn't shake the image of Aaron's vacant eyes. They haunted him. Accused him. Begged him to find Aaron's murderer. He looked over Hank's shoulders toward the students in the parking lot. A loud cheer had erupted as the cheer squad jumped into a routine. Something about an upcoming party next week.

Nate turned and met Hank's gaze. "I have my answer," Nate said bitterly. "Everyone has moved on."

Hank's expression darkened as though a cloud passed over his face. "When a young person dies, most people want to move on. They want to forget that it ever happened. That something like that won't touch them or those they love. They are grieving. Count on it. My question to you is…what will you do?"

"I don't know."

"Honesty. A good place to start. But that's not why I'm here. Not surprised about the ravens coming to your aid. They are loyal protectors for those they feel a connection with. Isn't that a raven pendant you wear?"

Nate fingered the silver image of a raven in flight that hung from a metal chain around his neck. "It was a gift from my dad on my twelfth birthday. Some nonsense about it connecting to our heritage."

"It's not nonsense, and you don't believe it is either, otherwise you would have pawned it or thrown it in the trash the day he left. I understand the ravens' reaction. It's the ghost's reaction I can't figure out."

A bell for class blasted over the parking lot's sound system, with the expected reaction. It sent students from the inner circles dashing toward the school's entrance. There was plenty of time. This was just the first bell.

"We'll talk later," Hank said. "I need to get inside. Take care and know that you are not alone. I heard Aaron's funeral is this weekend. Will you be there?"

He couldn't breathe. "I'll be there," he managed.

"Good." Hank stood, backing into the shadows again, leaving as silently as he had appeared.

Nate shut his eyes, squeezing down the pain that had gripped his heart like an iron fist when Hank mentioned Aaron's funeral. That word made it final. Permanent. An end. Nate would skip school. No one expected him to be here anyway. But they would think it was because he was afraid to show his face, not because he was torn up about Aaron's death. No, they'd create this story that he had murdered his best friend and gotten away with it.

Nate pressed his lips together. "Hell with it."

He grabbed his backpack, locked the door of his Jeep, and headed to class. If he hustled, he'd make it before the final bell. That would be a first.

"There you are," Ruth Ann said as she fast-walked toward him, looping her arm in his. Her face was flushed, which brought out her freckles, and her short hair was still damp from early morning swim practice. Today she wore a pink polka-dot sweater over a green striped skirt. They had been friends since grammar school, and it was good to see her. She always brightened his day. She pressed a folded paper onto his chest.

Nate grabbed it before it fell. "Am I supposed to know what this is?"

"It's a flyer for a party. There is this once-in-a-lifetime total lunar eclipse next Thursday and the cheerleaders thought they'd turn it into a celebration of Aaron's life."

He handed the flyer back to her. "I'm not going."

"Of course you're going. Carl said you wouldn't want to go, and I told him that was silly and that I would make sure you went. Carl would have been here to meet you before school too, but he had a tutoring session with his math teacher."

She was talking about normal things, and he couldn't do it. It felt as though the world was crashing down around him. "Look, I'm late anyway. I think I'm just going to skip school."

"Well, you can't. They're expecting you to skip. I overheard the principal talking to the office manager, Mrs. Cherry, about you. Mrs. Cherry mumbled that she was surprised they hadn't thrown you in jail. She said the cause of Aaron's death was unresolved and you were still a suspect."

Nate tensed, swearing under his breath. "Unresolved? Unresolved? Aaron was murdered. That sounds pretty *resolved* to me."

Ruth Ann smoothed her hand over his arm. "You are getting angry."

"No shit."

"That won't help catch whoever killed Aaron."

"You believe me?"

Her chin rose a notch higher. "Why wouldn't I?"

"I claimed that a ghost saved me from the killers. Everyone thinks I'm a nut case."

She laughed softly, shaking her head. "Ever since I can remember, students and teachers have avoided me because I was different. At first it was because of how I looked, and they called me 'chunky,' which was another way of saying 'fat.' When I had pneumonia and lost weight, they said I was too thin. The worst was when they realized I was smart. But you never treated me differently. Not ever. Not once. So, when I heard that you said you'd seen a ghost, I believed you. It is that simple."

Nate focused on Ruth Ann, who stood calmly at his side. Occasionally, students would nod to her as they passed by on their way to class. She acknowledged them, like someone might acknowledge a person you had met once and couldn't remember their name. She really didn't have many close friends, but everyone knew who she was and didn't ignore her outright. That was the consequence, he supposed, of Ruth Ann being the smartest person in school. Everyone at Pinedale High figured she'd be a big-time lawyer, maybe a Supreme Court Justice, cure cancer, or invent an AI that would take over the world. Most of his classmates were smart enough to realize that being mean to someone like Ruth Ann might come back to bite them. But then there were those who were as dumb as rocks and thought it would be a clever idea to tease her. That's where he came in. If she needed muscle to protect her, he was her guy.

"What are you thinking about?" She peered up at him.

"Nothing. You know me. My mind's a blank wall."

She pulled a face, rolling her eyes. "Why do you do that? You pretend you are as dumb as a dead pile of leaves. Pretend all you want to the others at school. That's your choice. But not to me. Are we clear?"

"Crystal," he said with a grin.

Chapter Eight

Two ravens circled over the granite mausoleum that stood like a beacon on the tallest hill in the Pinedale cemetery. The day of the funeral had arrived without a cloud in the sky.

Through wars, protests, and court challenges, Pinedale Cemetery had prevailed for hundreds of years in its coveted position on a series of rolling hills that overlooked a small forest, Raven Lake, and the high school. These lands had been owned by one of the founding fathers, who had bequeathed them to the town upon his death when North Carolina was still a colony.

The ravens dipped their wings and flew toward Nate, who had isolated himself in the shadows under a canopy of trees.

Nate stood observing the funeral ceremony from a distance. Aaron was being buried in a newer part of the cemetery. In the cemetery's heart stood headstones, granite mausoleums, and statues of angels, most dating back centuries. He bristled as late arrivals of brightly dressed mourners hurried to gather around Aaron's grave. He doubted any of the students were friends of Aaron. They had nothing better to do on a Saturday afternoon.

It wasn't right. The sun shouldn't be shining the day of his friend's funeral. It should be raining and the sky as black as his mood and the cemetery's wrought iron gates.

A priest finished muttering final words and people threw flowers onto Aaron's casket and watched it being lowered into the grave. At the assembly on Friday, Principal Kouriki had told the school that Aaron wouldn't have wanted his friends to dress in dark colors. Well, that showed how much she knew.

Death was not a happy event in the fall of your junior year in high school. Black was about the only color that fit the occasion.

Nate's lean build fit into his father's dark suit perfectly, and Nate matched it with the drabbest tie he could find. His shoulder-length black hair was secured by a leather tie at the nape of his neck and only the storm raging in his brown eyes disrupted his calm appearance. He didn't know why his mother had saved his dad's things for five years, but he was glad. He knew his choice of clothes would please Aaron. This was not a party; it felt like the end of the world.

"Nate," a feminine voice from the crowd yelled, slicing through his dark mood.

It never failed, he thought, as he watched a long-legged blonde walk over to where he stood. He wouldn't have been surprised if she had worn her head cheerleader's uniform to the funeral. She and her group of followers were never around when he needed company, only when he wanted to be left alone. It must be some sort of sick rule.

"Nate, isn't it terrible," she sniffled, and her blue eyes filled with tears. There was a time when the sight would have melted him into a puddle. Those days were long gone. A big fat tear traveled down her perfect cheek. "Imagine finding Aaron hanging from a rope. It must've been awful. Was it true that you pulled him down?"

Nate ground his teeth together. Her words conjured up the image of Aaron he had tried to block out for the past few days. It would have to be Cindy Fremont who brought everything back in a rush.

Dressed head to toe in the flashiest name brands money could buy, with a model's body, Cindy was almost every male student's fantasy.

He and Aaron had fought over her. Aaron had lost the fight but won the girl. And now Aaron was dead.

"I don't believe what everyone is saying about you," Cindy whispered.

Nate ignored her attempt at support. She was the kind of girl who would end up believing what she was told was the truth.

He stuck his hands in his pockets, nodding in the direction of a guy who was heading straight toward them. "I see you're back with your ex," Nate said.

It was Pete Hinkle, a football player who looked like an advertisement for a sports magazine. Cindy had dumped him when she'd seen him with a sophomore.

Cindy glanced over her shoulder. "I don't know what I would have done after Aaron died if it weren't for Hinkle." She sighed dramatically as Pete reached her side, putting his arm possessively around her shoulders. "I was so lonely."

Nate's anger bubbled unchecked to the surface. "Couldn't you wait until Aaron was buried before you started up with Hinkle again? Aaron really loved you."

"And what about you, Collier?" Hinkle interrupted. "Everyone knew you were in love with Cindy, especially Aaron. I heard the police were interested in the fight you and Aaron had. Do you think they know it was over Cindy?"

"We agreed we wouldn't mention the police at Aaron's funeral," Cindy pleaded.

"It was your idea," Hinkle accused. "I never agreed to anything."

"Back off, Hinkle," Nate shot back.

Cindy moved in between them. "Calm down. Both of you. Aaron is dead. We must stop treating each other like this. I keep thinking of the last time I saw him. He and I..." Her chin trembled as she glanced away. She brushed a tear from her face and turned back to Nate with a smile that looked forced. "We are all meeting in town at Irene's Café today. We're planning a memorial service to honor Aaron during the total lunar eclipse on Thursday. You should come."

She was trying. He'd give her that much. "Thanks, but I'll pass."

Hinkle held up his hands in disgust. "Cindy. You must be joking. Didn't you hear what I said? Collier is a suspect in Aaron's murder."

Nate turned away from the squabbling couple to walk toward his Jeep parked along the curb. They were perfect for each other, and so absorbed in their own lives they hadn't noticed he hadn't said goodbye.

He found it hard to believe he'd fought so hard to be accepted by these people. To be like them. Aaron told him he didn't fit in, but then neither had his dead friend. Of course, that was before Cindy decided she was bored with football players and started looking at the cross-country runners.

Aaron was easy for a girl to pick out, Nate remembered. He made running three miles look like a walk in the park. He always came in first.

Cindy liked the guys who came in first.

Nate was so deep in thought he jumped when someone stepped into the middle of his path.

"Did I startle you?" A man in a dark suit asked, showing Nate a badge.

The man looked like every C.I.A. or F.B.I. agent Nate had ever seen in the movies or on TV. He wore a dark, nondescript suit, white shirt, and unimaginative tie. Add to that a short military haircut, bland facial features, and a condescending smile. But something wasn't right. Something was off.

Just what he needed to make this day complete, more questions, Nate thought.

"The name's Detective Tom Henshaw, but you can cut out the title and call me Tom. I saw you run the other day. You ran like you had something to prove, first place, congratulations."

Nate shrugged. "Thanks, but the competition wasn't that great."

"Of course, Aaron was out of the picture."

Nate eyed the detective warily, noting what had bothered him earlier. He recognized the tie. It had belonged to Aaron. "I wouldn't kill someone just to win a lousy race."

"Course not, son." Henshaw smiled. "Relax, I didn't mean to imply you murdered the boy. Just wanted to say you ran well." He took out a leather-bound notepad and continued. "I just have a few questions about the death of your friend. Is this a good time?"

Nate looked at the determination on the detective's face. He knew instinctively the man didn't care if this was a good time for questions or whether Nate had run a good race. The guy wanted his questions answered. Still, Henshaw might be the type who could be flexible.

"I just watched my best friend being buried," Nate said, feeling like a part of him lay beside Aaron under the dirt.

"I'm sorry. Nevertheless," Henshaw said in a rush of words, "there are a few things about this case that don't add up. I'm of the opinion that it's easier to get information while it's still fresh in the mind. Don't you agree?"

So much for the flexibility theory. Nate sighed. He felt like someone had drained all the blood from his body, leaving only the shell. He remembered seeing a cartoon picture in health class about what the body would look like without a skeletal structure. Nate could relate to that image.

He watched Henshaw look over the scribbling in his notepad. Nate didn't recognize Henshaw as any of the policemen who had interrogated him. It meant either they were bringing in an expert to crack the case or this guy was doing some detective work on his own. Either way, Nate was too tired to care.

"Look, Detective, I really would like to help, but this isn't a good time." Nate turned and walked toward his Jeep. If the police are so interested in me, he thought, they can question me later. If he didn't get away from the cemetery, away from Aaron's grave, he knew he would lose the slender thread of control he held onto. The questions would have to wait. He had to escape.

He marched through the cemetery's iron gates at a pace he hoped would leave the detective in his dust. But he had to slow down and wait his turn to cross a wooden footbridge over a dried-up creek bed before heading in the direction of the parking lot.

Nate managed to reach his pewter-gray Jeep before

the detective caught up with him.

"I said I need to talk to you, son."

"I'm not your son." Nate struggled to remain calm. "You asked me if this was a good time. It's not. How do you know Aaron?"

The detective straightened. "I'm his uncle. How'd you guess?"

"The tie. Aaron's mother bought it for him. He hated it, said it made him look like an old man."

Henshaw smoothed the tie and put his hand on Nate's arm. "You're not making this easy on yourself."

Nate jerked his arm free of Henshaw's grasp. "That's exactly what all the other detectives kept telling me when I answered their questions. They all came to the same conclusion. They think I murdered Aaron."

"And did you?"

Chapter Nine

"I didn't kill Aaron. How many times must I tell you people?"

"Until you make us believers." Henshaw flipped through the pages of his notebook. "Ah, yes, here we are. You told Detective Morrison that you struggled with Aaron's killers when they tried to hang you. That would explain the bruising on your neck. Course, it could have been the struggle with Aaron that caused your injuries."

Nate met the detective's gaze. "Aaron was already dead when I found him."

"So you said." Henshaw nodded before returning to his notes. "Now, let's see. Oh yes, here's the good part. You escaped the murderers when a ghost appeared. And according to you, it was a ghost that saved lives. Now there's a twist."

Nate closed his eyes, wishing he could wake up from this nightmare. He knew it looked bad. No one believed him. Usually, that didn't bother him...or bother him that much. This was different. How could anyone believe he had killed his best friend?

Of course, it didn't help that he and Aaron had fought over Cindy in front of the whole school. The substitute counselor, Roger Williams, had finally broken up the fight. A visit to the principal, which resulted in a three-day suspension for both him and Aaron.

Suspension from school was not a new experience,

Nate recalled with a resigned sigh. He had lost count of the times he'd been suspended for skipping school, fights, or whatever. If there was any trouble at school, he was the first person the principal looked for. It had been different for Aaron. He had never been suspended and he took it pretty hard. Aaron worried it might jeopardize his chance for a college track scholarship.

"I'm asking you a question," Henshaw snapped, intruding on Nate's thoughts. "Where did you get the rope? It's the type used by rock climbers."

"Good to know, except I don't climb mountains. And how many times do I have to tell you I didn't kill Aaron? Are you going to arrest me?" Nate demanded, jerking open the door to his Jeep.

"One more question. Do you think your friend was capable of taking his own life?"

"You're nuts," Nate raised his voice, anger bubbling below the surface. "First you accuse me of murder, and then you suggest Aaron committed suicide."

Nate jumped into the Jeep. His hands shook as he started the engine. He needed to get away from this place, away from the memories that threatened to bury him alive. He looked in the rearview mirror, but the detective was just standing on the curb, watching him leave.

A loud vibrating sound caught his attention and he realized someone was pounding on his Jeep. He turned in the direction of the noise. "What the…"

"Let us in."

It was Carl, one of Nate's closest friends since grammar school. Carl jumped into the passenger's seat as Ruth Ann opened the back rear door, shoved books and a gym bag aside, and climbed in. It made sense that they wouldn't let him be alone on a day like today. But how could he explain to them that he *wanted* to have privacy?

Nate's eyes prickled and he had to blink and glance away. He didn't want anyone to see him cry. He had kept a tight hold on his feelings all through the funeral service and when they had lowered Aaron's coffin into the grave. He had shown little outward sign of emotion, other than clearing his throat. No tears. Screams of injustice. Calls for revenge. Nothing. He had been a statue.

But now his friends had arrived, and holding back took every ounce of willpower he possessed. It wasn't that they would make fun of him if he started to wail like a banshee. They wouldn't. This was all on him. He feared that if he gave in to the grief, he would lose his edge to find Aaron's killer and do what he needed to do to avenge his death. He hadn't realized that these two friends had attended Aaron's funeral, but he should have known. They would have been there, not just for Aaron but to support him.

Because of his size, kids at school had nicknamed Carl *Man Mountain*, and the football coach promised that next year he'd elevate Carl to varsity. Right after Nate's dad left, Carl's father invited Nate to go fishing with them on Raven Lake. Nate had accepted, but sitting for hours waiting for the fish to bite didn't suit him. Fishing wasn't for him, but he had appreciated the effort to include him. Carl's parents were like that. With Carl, everything was right or wrong, black or white. No gray area, which was why Carl and Aaron had gotten along so well. They both viewed life as a win-or-lose situation.

Nate, on the other hand, was all about the shades of

gray. His mother called his view on life nuanced. It was a fancy word for saying that nothing was ever the way it seemed.

He glanced in the rearview mirror. Predictably, Ruth Ann was putting his pile of schoolbooks into order, according to his schedule. Chemistry was first period, English Lit second period, and so on. She was like that. She liked order—everything in its place. She wore her hair close-cropped and spiky, and changed the color as often as some people changed their socks. Today her hair was blue, Aaron's favorite color.

Everything about her, except her hazel-green eyes, was petite. Usually, she wore bright layers of clothes, in plaids and stripes. But because of the funeral she'd worn black. Carl and Aaron thought wearing layers was because she couldn't decide what she wanted to wear. Nate disagreed. She'd never regained the weight she lost when she had been sick and wanted to hide the fact that she was so thin. She wanted to fit in, which was impossible when you had been classified as a genius in third grade.

Funny how he was noticing more about her lately. He supposed it had to do with Aaron's death. His friends were more important to him, since he'd lost Aaron.

He draped his arm over the back of his seat to include both Carl and Ruth Ann when he spoke, steeling his voice to sound strong. "I know what you're doing, and I'm grateful, but I'd like to be alone."

"Told ya," Carl said, glancing toward Ruth Ann in the back seat. "He wants his space, and we should honor his wishes. We can take him to the shop later. Can't say that I blame him for wanting privacy. This whole thing, Aaron dying, thinking Nate was somehow involved, is borderline insane."

Ruth Ann folded her hands in her lap. "Carl Amadeus Wilson. You are the one who is borderline if you think we're leaving Nate alone." She focused on Nate. "Don't give me that look. I'm not moving from this spot, and you can't make me."

"Of course I can make you. You're tiny, you barely reach my shoulders, and you weigh next to nothing. My gym bag weighs more than you. I want to be alone with my thoughts."

"See…" Carl said.

Ruth Ann waved Carl's comment away and jutted out her chin, crossing her arms over her chest. "Friends don't abandon friends. We are not leaving, and you know how I can get when I set my mind to do something. Or in this case, *not* do something. You should not be alone. None of us should be. And as for your thoughts—if left alone, they go to a dark place."

Nate held Ruth Ann's gaze for a few seconds. He knew that look. She was right. She never gave up once she set her mind. She was like a dog with a bone. He smiled to himself. He'd never tell her that analogy. She wouldn't appreciate the comparison. She was a cat person. She never gave up on her friends, no matter the cost. It was one of the things he liked about her.

He felt that prickling sensation behind his eyes and turned back to the steering wheel. "Ruth Ann. You are annoying. Why do I put up with you?"

"You know you love me. Less chatter. More driving. I'm starving. Is anyone hungry?"

Carl's eyes grew as big as saucers. "I'm hungry. We should go to Irene's Café afterwards."

Nate shoved the keys into the ignition. "It's a

conspiracy. Okay, you both win. Buckle up. Carl mentioned you wanted to take me to a shop in town. Not sure what that's about, or how it relates, but I'm game. What's it called?"

"Ghost Whisperer," Ruth Ann said. "I'm hoping we'll find answers to why Aaron was killed."

Chapter Ten

Nate parked his Jeep along a side street in Pinedale's Old Town, wondering how he'd allowed Ruth Ann to talk him into this absurd wild goose chase. He'd never admit to her that she had been right. If left to his own devices, he would have most certainly spent the day sinking deeper and deeper into dark thoughts.

The Ghost Whisperer store was tucked into a narrow alley, flanked by three-story weathered red-brick buildings. A bronze plaque dated the alley back to the early seventeen hundreds and claimed it was the location of the first ghost sighting. Shops—selling ghost-themed jewelry and clothes, pink and purple rock-salt crystal lamps, and potions, tinctures, and powders, guaranteed for a successful ghost exorcism—lined the cobblestone streets.

Ruth Ann led the way, opened the door to the Ghost Whisperer, and was greeted by the sound of windchimes and tinkling bells. At first glance the store looked no larger than his bedroom. The ceiling was painted midnight blue with tiny lights representing what looked like constellations. The shop's shelves were crowded with figurines, crystals, stacks of books, and rows of jewelry.

A woman, leaning on a wooden cane painted with symbols of animals, moved around the counter to them. Her white braid circled her head like a crown, and she wore a gold tunic, embroidered with silver half-moons and stars, over black leggings. She smiled and opened her arms in a welcome embrace and hugged Ruth Ann. "I haven't seen you in so long. To what do I owe the pleasure?"

"Mrs. Waters, I'd like to introduce you to my friends, Nate and Carl. We have questions regarding ghost sightings at the high school."

"Oh, my," Mrs. Waters said, nodding toward Nate. "You're the one who found his friend on the football field. I am so sorry. Would you like a cup of peppermint tea? I made a fresh pot."

Nate knew this sort of tactic well. If you wanted to avoid answering a question, you changed the subject. "Thank you for the offer of tea, but we are here to learn what you might know about ghosts."

Mrs. Waters returned to the counter and picked up her mug, tracing her finger over the rim. "According to your school's principal, there are no such things as ghosts, and she would not approve of you being here. Some say that ghosts are only figments of a person's imagination."

Nate moved to the counter. "Your shop literally says, *Ghost Whisperer*, and everything in here shouts that you believe ghosts are real. And you're holding a mug with an image of a ghost hovering over a tombstone. We just want to ask you a few questions."

Mrs. Waters set the mug aside with a sigh. "You speak your mind. That is not easy to do at your age. I could get into a lot of trouble if I talk to you about them. My shop, and the stores along this street, are tolerated because they bring in a lot of tourist revenue for the town. But the mayor, the superintendent, and your principal made it clear that if any Pinedale High School students frequented my shop, I was instructed to discourage them, or they would shut me down."

"And yet, you're telling us the one thing that would make us even more curious," Ruth Ann said. "You're saying that people are trying to keep the existence of ghosts a secret."

Mrs. Waters took another sip of her tea. "Perhaps the people I mentioned are concerned the sightings will cause a panic."

Carl had been investigating figurines of ghosts on a shelf and looked over. "Nate, tell Mrs. Waters that the man who attacked you had red eyes. That can't be normal, and it wasn't mentioned in the newspaper."

"Oh, dear." Mrs. Waters' hands trembled as she poured herself more tea. It spilled over the rim onto the counter. She ignored the water as she lifted her gaze. "It's happening again."

An ivory candlestick holder, shaped like a ghost, toppled to the ground and crashed on the stone floor. Shards of pottery scattered in all directions.

"Sorry." Carl bent to pick up the pieces. "Sorry. That was me being clumsy. Do you have a broom? I'd be happy to clean it up."

Mrs. Waters hurried over to Carl and knelt beside him. "Do not worry about the mess. I have at least a dozen of these candlestick holders in the back room. They are very popular and reasonably priced. My daughter, Louisa, will take care of it. I don't want you to cut your hands." She stood, glancing at a clock on the wall shaped like a haunted house. "Oh, dear, where has the time gone? I'm expecting my séance group within the hour. Perhaps you all could come back later? Louisa, could you come in here for a minute?"

Nate glanced toward Ruth Ann and Carl. They all seemed to share the same panicked expression. Mrs. Waters was changing the subject again. They couldn't let her do that.

As though reading his mind, Ruth Ann stepped forward. "You don't need to bother Louisa. We'd be happy to help. Many hands make light work."

Nate nodded a thank you to Ruth Ann and grabbed a broom he'd seen leaning against the back counter, recognizing that Ruth Ann had more than cleaning up in mind. They'd help with the cleanup and maybe coax Mrs. Waters into telling them more about what she meant when she'd said, "It's happening again." An ominous warning if ever he'd heard one.

Louisa, a girl maybe a year younger than Ruth Ann, with a mass of tight curls, poked her head out from the back room. "Do you need me, Mama?"

"It's all under control, sweetheart, but thank you. Could you call Mrs. Stuart and remind her that the séance begins within the hour? She always forgets. Now, where was I?"

Nate used the broom to sweep the broken candlestick holder into a pile. "You mentioned that what I described may have happened before."

"So I did. I thought…hoped this day would never come." Mrs. Waters walked over to a bookshelf. She selected a book and dusted off the spine with a handkerchief she slipped out of her sleeve. "This will help. It's a partial history of the ghosts of Pinedale. It's incomplete, as the publisher went out of business before the books were released to the public. There was a fire and all, but a few books were recovered."

"I'm not much of a reader," Carl said, grabbing a dustpan to help Nate sweep up the mess on the floor. "How about the short version?"

Her mouth moved in a half-smile that didn't reach her eyes, as she hugged the book to her chest. "I also like the shorter versions. Before the school was built on its present-day location, there was a lengthy list of ghost sightings. Not surprising because even before North Carolina became a state this was a turbulent and violent area. When a person dies tragically or before their time, they have difficulty moving on to their afterlife. With no other choice left for them, they become ghosts. As a result, our small town became known as one of the most haunted on the Eastern seaboard."

"Not very cool for the ghosts that they couldn't move on," Carl said. "Good for tourism, like you said."

Mrs. Waters hmphed. "You must remember that those were very superstitious times. The worst hauntings were around the MacGregor mansion, which was built long before Pinedale High School existed. There was even speculation of possession. Something had to be done, but it was tricky, as the mansion was owned by one of the founding fathers. It was only when he died that action was taken. The townspeople of Pinedale thought by covering up its ruins they could contain the ghosts. I worried when they started the excavation this summer that they might awaken the evil the town worked so hard to destroy."

"Why didn't you say something?" Ruth Ann asked.

"Who would have believed me? The evil I mentioned happened hundreds of years ago."

Nate swept the pile of broken pottery into the dustpan Carl held for him and dumped it into the waste basket. "Why were the people in town so afraid of the ghosts?"

Mrs. Waters put the book on the counter, staring at it for a while before she continued. "The ghosts were vengeful. There were mysterious incidents, such as a collapsed ceiling that buried the family inside, and a fire that destroyed the buildings on Beeker Street."

Nate exchanged glances with his friends. It was as though they were all having the same thoughts. "That is awful, but those kinds of tragic events aren't that uncommon. Even today with building codes and fire departments, accidents like that can occur. You said this happened hundreds of years ago, and from what our history teacher told us, the seventeenth and eighteenth centuries were superstitious times. People often blamed what they couldn't explain on witches and supernatural creatures like demons, goblins, and ghosts."

Mrs. Waters crossed to stand behind the counter as though using it as a barrier between herself and Nate, Ruth Ann, and Carl. "True. All true." Then with a deep breath she reached under the counter and pulled out a leather-bound book tied shut with a faded black ribbon. "Back then, there were those who thought as you do. They had heard of the witch trials in Salem and did not want to repeat the hysteria that had gripped that town and resulted in the murder of innocents. They did not want to believe in ghosts that could kill or serial killers who could inhabit a living person's body." Mrs. Waters shoved the leather-bound book toward Nate. "But they couldn't deny that the only people who had been targeted had a connection to what is now the Pinedale High School property. One of my ancestors recorded it all in detail. In the book are dates, names, and events where someone died, and the plan the townspeople devised to imprison the ghosts. What he learned was that the more the person resists possession, the faster their body burns out."

Carl threw up his arms. "Imprison ghosts? Lady, you had me right up until that part. You can't lock up a ghost. They'd walk right through the walls. Next, you're going to try and sell us one of the amulets in your shop. This whole thing is a con. I'm not sure why ghosts are on the loose, but Ruth Ann has a theory that one might be responsible for our friend's death. All we need from you is to figure out how we can prove that theory to the police, because they're trying to pin the murder on Nate."

"And why," Ruth Ann said, "did they think just covering up the cemeteries and mansions where the ghosts haunted would work?"

"They didn't. But the townspeople were desperate, and it was a gamble. They needed to prevent the serial killer ghost, which they called the Nuckelavee, from terrorizing the land where Pinedale High School is now located. And inexplicably, it worked. Maybe it was a coincidence, and the ghosts moved. Or they dealt with the most violent of their numbers. Whatever the cause, something changed when the site was uncovered again. As for the amulets..." Mrs. Waters smiled. "They have been used for thousands of years in one form or another to protect against evil spirits. People love their charms, and there is power and comfort in believing something can protect you. Nate wears the image of a raven. A powerful symbol. It represents wisdom, intelligence, and transformation. I remember the day Nate's father bought it for him."

"You knew my father?"

The chimes over the door sang out as a swarm of men and women poured into the shop, all ages and sizes, dressed for warmth. Some dove straight for the shelves of jewelry, others clustered around figurines, while a few headed toward Mrs. Waters.

"That would be my séance group, children. We can resume this discussion later. Or, if you would like, I can conduct one for you. Unless, of course, one of you has already seen your friend."

"About that," Ruth Ann said. "I saw Aaron yesterday. He's the one who suggested we visit the Ghost Whisperer."

"Mrs. Waters," a woman said, interrupting. Her salt-and-pepper hair had been swept behind her ears, and she wore a gray tailored suit. She sounded quite businesslike. "I am sorry to interrupt, but we should get started. You said this would be a good time? I'm anxious to speak with my husband and find out where he hid the will."

Mrs. Waters patted the middle-aged woman's hand. "Of course, Mrs. Kennith. Gather your friends and we will begin at once." She turned toward Nate, Ruth Ann and Carl. "I really must tend to my group. There is a wonderful café nearby. It has been lovely meeting you all."

Chapter Eleven

The lightly sweet, yeasty, and buttery aromas of baking bread combined with the scents of vanilla, cinnamon, and apple as Nate settled down in a corner booth of Irene's Café, his stomach rumbling. He fingered the raven pendant to take his mind off his hunger and that Ruth Ann had seen Aaron's ghost. Why her and not him?

The selfish thought caught him off guard. Talking about ghosts and spirits and things that went bump in the night was making him nuts. Then he fingered the raven pendant again. What had his father been doing visiting Mrs. Waters' shop? He got the impression that it had not been the first time. It made sense that his father had purchased the pendant at her shop. But why the image of a raven?

He remembered his father mentioning that he believed his ancestors were descended from an indigenous tribe that lived in the area over two hundred years ago. When he questioned his father later, he'd said it was centuries ago, and the records had been lost. Soon after, his father left.

Nate caught another whiff of fresh-baked bread and his stomach growled again. He had told his friends he was too anxious to eat, but the café's smells had triggered his hunger…and his memories.

He, his father, and his mother would visit Irene's every Sunday after church. They always ordered the same thing. The café was famous for their huge cinnamon rolls, smothered in frosting—the size of dinner plates. His family would share a cinnamon roll, and the waitress would bring them three forks. When his father left, he had never wanted to return to the café, but his mother had insisted. She said it was a way for them to keep the memory of Nate's father alive. She made it sound as though his dad was dead.

They'd had a terrible argument. The angrier Nate grew, the calmer his mother became. Nate had said his father wasn't dead. He had abandoned them. There was a difference. In the end, she said she understood his frustration, but that he had to do this for her. And he had.

The café was crowded today with some of the same people Nate had seen at the funeral service. Cindy and Hinkle were grouped around a large center table with at least a dozen of their friends. Everyone talked at once, alternating between posing for pictures and laughing at some joke. It was like lunch time in the cafeteria. The popular kids had co-opted the largest table and made it their own.

The last thing he wanted was to connect with more people.

Carl and Ruth Ann circumvented Cindy and Hinkle's table, avoiding eye contact, as they wound their way toward Nate. But as Ruth Ann walked past, Cindy reached out toward her and whispered in her ear. Ruth Ann nodded, then resumed her way to Nate's table.

Ruth Ann placed their giant cinnamon roll in the center of the table, slid in next to Nate in the booth, and sliced the roll into three equal sections. "*Bon appétit!*"

Nate glanced toward Cindy, noting that she was staring at them. She looked pale and her eyes were red and swollen as though she had been crying. "What did Cindy have to say?"

"Only that she was sorry about Aaron."

He glanced in Cindy's direction again, but she had resumed talking with Hinkle. "She has a heart. Who knew?" He reached for a plate for his portion of the cinnamon roll and a fork. "Thank you for this, but it wasn't necessary. I told you I wasn't hungry."

Carl took one of the sections of the cinnamon roll and put it onto his plate. "We heard your stomach complaining clear across the room."

"When were you going to tell us about seeing Aaron's ghost?" Nate asked.

Ruth Ann scooped up her section of the cinnamon roll without using a fork and licked frosting from her fingers. "Until Mrs. Waters said something, I wasn't sure I would. I'm still thinking that I didn't see what I thought I saw."

Nate swallowed, nodding. He could relate. He still questioned if seeing the ghost the day Aaron was killed was real or something he imagined. "That's fair. Admitting that you've seen a ghost is wild. Where did you see Aaron?"

"Aaron was by the locker bays," Ruth Ann said. "I had the feeling he was looking for something."

"At school?" Carl said.

She took another bite. "I thought it strange, as well."

"Okay," Nate said. "Let's go."

"Where are we going?" Carl said.

Nate shrugged. "Why, to break into the school, of course."

Carl laughed. "Does anyone see the irony of Nate wanting to break *into* school? He's usually the first one out the door."

Ruth Ann whacked Carl on the arm with the book Mrs. Waters had given them. "That is not nice. When you were struggling in school, none of us teased you, saying that you weren't smart. You are doing much better on your test scores now, thanks to Assistant Coach Riley's afterschool tutoring program. So you, more than anyone, should know how it feels when people don't think you have a brain."

Carl glanced between Nate and Ruth Ann, rubbing his arm, frowning. "You're right. Sorry, Nate."

"No need to apologize. I have a reputation as the town's screw-up to protect."

Ruth Ann pointed the book toward Nate. "Enough. Stop doing that. The both of you. You tease each other about not being good enough, or smart enough, or handsome…"

"Did Ruth Ann suggest that we're not handsome?" Nate said, grinning. "I'm crushed." He nodded toward Carl.

"I think she was talking about you," Carl said with a mouthful of cinnamon roll. "I'm a catch."

She jutted out her chin as her eyes brimmed with unshed tears. "You are both hideous," she said, her voice catching on the last word. "I never said either of you weren't handsome. You tease each other about looking like trolls. I can't bear it. Aaron is gone. I keep hoping this is all a terrible dream. I never got the chance to tell him how wonderful he was and how much his friendship meant to me. When I saw him, I thought…" She pressed her hand against her mouth.

Nate's chest tightened as he gathered Ruth Ann in his arms. He had been so caught up with his own grief he had not stopped to realize how his friends were feeling. "You are right. We'll do better. I promise. Won't we, Carl?"

Carl nodded, wiping his mouth with his napkin. "I'm sorry too."

Ruth Ann pushed away from Nate, drying her tears with a tissue. "Thank you. Both of you. Change of subject. Do you think I was just seeing Aaron at school because I missed him? That he wasn't really there at the locker bays, maybe he was a projection? A sensory experience or a coping mechanism that helped me deal with the enormity of his death."

In clinical terms, what she said made sense. Nate knew she wanted to see Aaron again. So did he and Carl, but as she sat there, looking so serious, and talking like the smart person that she was, her whole explanation made him smile. He chose his words carefully. No way would he tell her how cute she looked when she was using big words.

"I do not believe what you saw was a projection. It was Aaron, and you know that. Otherwise, you wouldn't have insisted we visit the Ghost Whisperer shop. I believe Aaron is trying to tell us something. He wants us to help him solve his murder."

She gifted Nate with a watery smile. "We can't break into school now. We must wait until it's dark."

Nate leaned against the table with a smirk. "Sensible. It's official. I've corrupted the smartest girl in school. What are people going to think about you breaking into Pinedale? If we are caught, it will ruin your perfect reputation. If we are suspended, that would go on your permanent record and jeopardize your chances of attending your parents' Ivy League alma mater."

Ruth Ann took a bite out of her cinnamon roll. "One can only hope."

Chapter Twelve

Hands shoved into his pockets; Nate entered the side entrance of the Pinedale Movie Theatre his mother owned. The marquee advertised a weekend matinee showing of old movies inspired by the work of Edgar Allan Poe: *The Tell-Tale Heart*, *The Bloodhound*, *The Murders in the Rue Morgue*, and *Two Evil Eyes*.

His mother was making popcorn by the counter. As usual, she was working alone. It cost money to hire staff.

"What can I do to help?"

She looked over her shoulder. "Oh, my, I didn't expect you here today. You should be with your friends. How are you doing?"

Nate went around the counter and grabbed a clean cloth to help wipe down the display case jammed with a variety of candy and soda pop. His mother was like that. She worked long hours, rarely saying she was tired, because she wanted her son to enjoy being a kid. How could he tell her that those days ended when his dad walked out on him.

He avoided her question. His mother meant well, but she had enough on her mind. She didn't need to worry about him. "It's all good. We were in Old Town together earlier. I'll meet up with them when the theater closes. I like your choice of matinee movies."

She smiled. "I thought you might. Your father was a Poe fan as well. *The Pit and the Pendulum* and the *Cask of Amontillado* are on backorder. I'm thinking that Edgar Allan Poe's movies might draw in the crowd. God knows we need the business. Horror is all the rage right now, and as you always say, Poe was one of the originals in that genre. Would you mind checking out the theater? I gave it a sweep, but it could use another. Oh, before you go. I received a call from the principal."

He reached for a broom from the broom closet, fortifying himself for grilling. The principal only called when he had done something wrong or failed a test. The conversation was always the same. This was Nate's junior year and if he expected to graduate and attend a university or a community college, he needed to bring up his grades. How could he tell her that he had no intention of attending college? She needed him here in Pinedale. There was no way she could run the theater on her own.

Each year got harder. People didn't go to the movies the way they used to, especially theaters like theirs that only had one screen and liked to show indie films and classics like the ones they were featuring this weekend.

His mother opened a carton of candy and began displaying it under the counter. "She called to ask how you were doing with Aaron's death. And then she asked the most curious question. She asked me if you still believed you saw a ghost the night of Aaron's murder."

Nate set his broom aside, reaching for the glass cleaner again. He concentrated on cleaning the display case and ducked his head to avoid his mother's gaze. She was worried, and the last thing he wanted was to worry her. "Everything happened so fast. I'm not sure what I saw anymore."

"Nate, honey, if you're sure? It's just that it brought back…"

"Brought back what? Exactly?"

"Probably nothing. I'm tired, and the young man we hired to run the projector called in sick. Would you mind operating the movie for me? We'll start with *The Murders in the Rue Morgue*."

A few hours later the last scene of that movie displayed moonlight mirrored on the water in a tree-lined park. The scene faded as the credits came on. Nate sat in the projection room at a table, taking notes. Should he watch the movie again? He had lost count of how many times he'd viewed it.

"There you are," Ruth Ann said, entering the projection room with Carl following close behind her. "No worries if you must work tonight. We can sneak into the school some other night."

"No, tonight is good." Nate closed his notebook and rose to check the projector. "I must have lost track of time."

"Were you doing homework?" Carl said, picking up the notebook Nate had left on the table.

"Better. I'm learning how to be a detective. Did you know this movie, *The Murders in the Rue Morgue*, was written as a story by Edgar Allan Poe in eighteen hundred and forty-one and has been described as the first modern detective story? This was way before Authur Conan Doyle wrote his first Sherlock Holmes book in eighteen hundred and eighty-seven."

Carl winked at Ruth Ann. "Your smarts are starting to rub off on our track star. I've never heard Nate say so many smart things in one paragraph before."

Ruth Ann narrowed her gaze toward Carl and shook her head slowly. "Carl. We talked about this. What did I say about this type of teasing?"

"Sorry. Old habit. But why the interest in detective stories suddenly?"

"I'm hoping it will help us solve Aaron's murder."

Chapter Thirteen

Nate parked his Jeep on the perimeter of the school grounds and a short distance from the excavation site.

"This is a bad idea," Carl said as he got out of the Jeep and held the door for Ruth Ann. "It's pitch black. Doesn't anyone worry about the fact that there's a killer on the loose? We shouldn't be doing this. We should leave the detective work for the police and that Detective Henshaw I saw you talking to at the cemetery."

Nate locked the doors of his Jeep, pocketing the keys. "What I learned watching that movie, *The Murders in the Rue Morgue*, is that sometimes detectives make assumptions about cases. They are so focused on the big picture they fail to notice things that are out of place, or missing, or just plain don't make any sense."

"Okay, Detective Collier," Carl said. "Or should I start calling you Sherlock? What are the police overlooking?"

"I'm not sure. We should focus on why Aaron is haunting the school's locker bays."

Ruth Ann wove a powder blue scarf with silver fringe around her neck, and buttoned her jacket. "I wouldn't say Aaron was haunting the lockers. He was just standing there, looking a little lost."

"I think this whole thing is a waste of time. You heard Mrs. Waters. It's possible a ghost killed Aaron. Stranger things have happened in this town, and Mrs.

Waters has a book to prove it."

"Carl has a point," Ruth Ann said.

Nate ducked under the low hanging branches of a maple tree. Was he taking on more than he could handle? He wasn't a detective, and the more he thought about Aaron's murder, the more questions he had than answers. Starting with why anyone would want to kill Aaron. He was like an invisible kid. Except for asking the head cheerleader out on a date, and winning races, he had never done anything to ruffle anyone's feathers. True, Hinkle might have been mad because Cindy had dumped him and agreed to date Aaron, but that shouldn't be a motive for murder, should it? What was he missing?

He motioned for Ruth Ann and Carl to join him as he headed across the football field toward the school building. "If we do have a murderous ghost at Pinedale High School, that's all the more reason to uncover who or what it is. Who's to stop them from killing again?"

"My point exactly," Carl said, raising his voice and jogging to keep up with Nate. "Which is why we should leave it to the police."

"Carl, if you want to stay here," Nate said, pausing to allow Carl to catch up with him. "You can stay outside if you want. Ruth Ann and I can sneak into the school and let you know what we find."

"Hey, you're not leaving me out here alone," Carl said. "Those flocks of ravens might like you, but they dive-bomb me whenever they have a chance."

"It's called a kindness, or a conspiracy of ravens, not a flock, and if you would share your lunch once in a while, they might warm up to you too." Nate jogged up the stairs to the back entrance and peered into the glass of the double doors of the school, then tried the door handle just in case the janitor had forgotten to lock it up. "It's unlocked. Let's go."

"Unlocked, and you don't think that's the least bit suspicious?" Carl said.

"Or a lucky accident," Ruth Ann added, joining Nate by the double doors. "Carl, are you coming?"

"Is the surface of some football fields composed of monofilament polyethylene-blended fibers tufted into a polypropylene backing?"

Ruth Ann laughed. "I'm impressed. That is a cool way to say yes," she added as she entered the school.

Nate jabbed Carl in the ribs as he held the door open for Ruth Ann. "Trying to impress the smartest girl in school?" he whispered to Carl as they entered the school and followed Ruth Ann to the junior class locker bays.

Carl just shrugged. "Maybe I am. She's cute in her own quirky way." Carl, hands in pockets, walked past Nate to catch up to Ruth Ann.

Nate frowned. Quirky? And what was Carl doing thinking of Ruth Ann in any way other than as a friend?

"Hurry up, Nate." Ruth Ann raised her arm and pointed down a corridor. "I think that's Aaron."

"I see him," Carl said. "Not so much see him. He looks all wavy and semi-transparent. But it's him. Wow. This is wild. I'm seeing ghosts. Who is he talking to?"

"Fiona," Nate said. "That's the ghost I told you about, the one who saved me from Aaron's killers. I wonder what she's doing here?"

Carl smoothed his hair back from his forehead. "You never said she was good-looking."

Ruth Ann narrowed her gaze toward Carl. "Behave. It looks like Aaron is trying to open his locker."

Nate stumbled back. His heart thundered in his chest

like it always did in the seconds before a race. He had told the police he'd seen a ghost, but in the days that followed, he'd been honest with his mother when he said he'd started to doubt himself.

But Ruth Ann and Carl saw not only Fiona but Aaron as well. Aaron still wore the same jogging clothes with the school's python logo on the sweatshirt as he had the night he'd died.

Nate clamped down on his jaw, as Aaron's body hanging from the goalpost flashed in his thoughts. He swallowed, clearing the lump in his throat.

He wanted to ask Aaron stupid, silly things, like did it bother him that he had to wear the sweatshirt and jogging pants for eternity? Because Aaron had made the track team, he had to wear the team's logo. The coaches didn't seem to care that Aaron was afraid of snakes.

Nate felt the pressure over his heart and rubbed his chest. Better not to bring up Aaron's fear of snakes under the circumstances. "Aaron. Do you know who killed you?"

Aaron whispered something to Fiona.

Fiona rested her hand on Aaron's arm in the same manner Ruth Ann did when she was attempting to calm him down. That must be a girl-thing. He knew it helped him. Did it work for Aaron as well?

"Aaron would prefer not to talk with a living just yet," Fiona said. "I am helping him with his transition; however, it is early days and there is still a lot of resentment and anger, as you might imagine." She paused when Aaron bent to whisper to her again. She nodded to him before continuing. "He told me to tell you not to trust anyone. He is also afraid the killers will murder again if they are not stopped."

Ruth Ann stepped forward. "Can you ask him what he was looking for? I noticed he was trying to open one of the lockers."

Aaron's image flickered as he bent to whisper to Fiona.

"Oh," Fiona said, her eyes widening.

Lights in the hallway flickered and one of them sputtered, spraying sparks overhead. Then Fiona and Aaron disappeared.

Carl whistled low. "That was weird."

"It was all weird," Ruth Ann said. "And troubling. I had the impression Aaron was afraid to tell us something. We are his friends."

"We need to start back where it all began," Nate said. "I think we're overlooking clues that might help us discover the reason Aaron was killed."

Carl grinned. "Okay, Sherlock, where and when do we start?"

"You're sticking with the nickname? Not sure how I feel about that, but if you and Ruth Ann are interested in helping solve Aaron's murder, we start tonight. We will check back in with our parents, and I'll meet you all back here after dinner. We can tell them we are all going to a special showing at my mom's theater."

"*Murder in the Rue Morgue?*" Ruth Ann said with a shiver. "I'd better tell my parents we're seeing a romantic comedy or they'll forbid me to go."

"They really don't know you very well," Nate said.

"They don't know me at all."

Chapter Fourteen

Later that night, with Carl in the passenger's seat, Nate drove toward the school. It turned out that Ruth Ann's parents were leaving for New York in the morning and wanted her with them tonight for a farewell dinner. He'd had to drive because Carl's beater car was in the shop again. This time it was to fix the brakes. Last week it had been the transmission.

Carl ran through a selection of CDs until he found the one he liked. The sounds rocked the Jeep with its intensity. Carl, lost in the music, thumped the dashboard in perfect rhythm with his fingers.

"Want to jam later?" Nate said over the pulsating sounds.

Carl nodded, without missing a beat.

Nate wanted to find out who killed Aaron. Not just to prove his own innocence, but to dispel the rumors that Aaron had committed suicide. He needed more information. He'd told his friends they needed to find clues, and that was accurate. But despite Carl calling him Sherlock, Nate was out of his depth. Reading Poe and Doyle, and watching old mystery and thriller movies, did not make him a detective. But he was motivated on many levels.

He wanted to find Aaron's killer, dispel the suicide rumors, and at the same time prove his own innocence. He told his friends it didn't matter to him that people thought he'd murdered his best friend. But it did. It mattered a lot.

Then there was the issue with Fiona. He wasn't sure how he felt about her. When Carl said she was good-looking, the comment struck a nerve. He had also thought her attractive and had spent way too much time thinking about her. He'd heard about that happening to people who were rescued. Her mother claimed that was what had happened to her when she met Nate's dad. She'd called it the Florence Nightingale Effect, or Nightingale Syndrome. It was when a person falls in love with someone who has saved them. In his mother's case, her car had caught fire, and his father was the firefighter who had dragged her out of the car before it exploded.

"I've been doing a lot of thinking since we saw Fiona and Aaron," Carl said. "I was talking to my Gran at dinner, and she said her great-grandmother told her about a legend of a serial killer ghost that sounded a lot like the story Mrs. Waters told us."

Nate stopped at a traffic light, waiting for it to change. "Did she have anything to say about the bones that were dug up? Everyone thinks it's an old cemetery. It also looks like some sort of metal roof over the mansion."

"Iron," Carl said. "Gran didn't know about the bones. Could have been a battlefield. The roof is made of iron, though. My Gran said it was nailed onto the roof to keep the ghosts who haunted the mansion prisoners. That's why cemetery gates are made of iron. It was believed to keep ghosts inside. In this case, it must have worked because there weren't many reports of ghosts until they started digging and removed part of the roof."

The light changed and Nate turned down the tree-lined street that led to the school. Branches swayed in the night air as shadows twisted across the road. "The ghosts couldn't have been happy as prisoners."

Carl switched off the music. "Gran was afraid. I could see it in her eyes. She told me one of the founding fathers of Pinedale built that mansion, the one the contractors dug up, in the late sixteen hundreds, before North Carolina even became a state. He built it from the ruins of a Scottish castle he had transported stone by stone across the Atlantic. According to Gran, there was a serial killer in Pinedale about that same time. The person was never caught, but the killing stopped around the time the man who had built the mansion died. The town's legend claimed the mansion was haunted by several ghosts: a cranky old man and his daughter, and a third that had been named the Nuckelavee. He's the one she believed was the serial killer. They found a portrait of the young girl with long red hair in the mansion and presumed it was the ghost's daughter, since at the time of the owner's death he was single and had had no children."

Nate turned in to the school's parking lot. "How did the daughter die?"

"They said she was strangled."

Chapter Fifteen

Nate was having doubts. For the first time Carl led the way to the excavation site on the football grounds in silence. Neither one of them thought this was a good plan, but here they were at the scene of the crime. It was a testament to how much they had valued their friend and wanted to find out who had murdered him.

The police had used yellow caution crime scene tape to keep the public out, which Nate and Carl ignored.

Carl peered down into the hole created by the construction crew. "At this time of night, it looks like a haunted castle, except for the iron roof that was removed."

"Hold on," Nate said, easily catching up to Carl. "I think I heard something."

"It sounded like someone broke a window or dropped a glass."

Nate knelt to inspect a ladder that led down to the bottom of the excavation pit. "Probably rats."

Carl rolled his eyes. "That makes me feel so much better. I'll bet it was the ghost."

Nate began descending the ladder. "Except all the ghosts I've heard of rattle chains. You coming?"

"Of course I am. Wait up."

The air got cooler as Nate descended. He calculated it was about two or three stories down. Carl was directly above him on the ladder. He had to hand it to his friend.

Nate knew he was afraid, but that hadn't stopped him.

Nate jumped down the last few rungs of the ladder to the ground. It was as dark as the inside of a cave, and filled with spider webs and sounds of things slithering in the shadows. Carl was right to call this place a haunted castle.

He switched on the flashlight app on his phone and the light illuminated a wooden door with a missing handle. Whoever had buried this castle hadn't wanted anyone getting inside.

He leaned his shoulder against the door, but it wouldn't budge.

"What the hell?" Carl shouted from a short distance away. "Was that a copperhead snake?"

Nate raised his voice. "They are more afraid of you than you are of them." Carl used a few swear words Nate knew neither of their moms would approve. "Hey, get over here and give me a hand. I found a door, but I can't get it opened."

Together they leaned against the door, but even adding Carl's strength didn't move it. It felt as solid and as unmovable as stone.

Carl drew back. "This is nuts. We're not getting in this way. This calls for a little mental power."

"You've already figured out another way in, haven't you?" Nate said, moving away from the door.

"This place is built like a castle. So, if you can't go in the front door of a building," Carl continued, "and the windows are boarded up. What is the next possibility?"

"You find the secret passageway." Nate smiled, motioning for his friend to follow him.

It was unbelievable, Nate thought to himself. Carl was identified with learning differences, yet he could solve complex puzzles in any given situation.

Nate led the way through a narrow space between the excavation wall and the castle. "Keep your flashlight app on. It's dark down here."

"And cold," Carl said. "I keep thinking about Aaron. When we saw him earlier tonight at the locker bays, he looked so sad. I wanted to give him a hug and tell him that it would be okay. But I couldn't because he's a ghost, and I couldn't tell him it would be okay because it's never going to be okay for him. This sucks. I'm so mad and frustrated. Whoever did this to him…"

Nate turned and reached out to grab Carl for a quick hug. "Yeah. I know exactly how you feel. I want to catch this creep too. That's what really keeps me going. When we saw Aaron, I realized he is stuck. If we find our friend's killer, maybe Aaron will move on to a place where he can be happy."

"I'm counting on it." Carl swiped at his eyes. "What is that over there? It looks like a passageway, but I'll never fit."

"I've got this. Maybe it widens. I'll let you know."

Nate ducked into a narrow passageway and inched his way forward.

"Find anything?" Carl yelled.

"The passageway keeps getting narrower," Nate shouted over his shoulder. 'No sense both of us getting stuck in here if I'm wrong. Wait fifteen, twenty minutes. If I haven't opened the door by then, go for help to break down the door from your end."

Nate heard Carl's protests as he slid his body along the narrow opening in the wall. Making his way in total darkness, he thanked his cross-country training that kept his body slim.

Sticky cobwebs clung to his face and the close quarters made it impossible for him to remove them. He estimated he'd gone about twenty feet when he felt a wintry blast of air on his face. The inky blackness enveloping him changed as he saw a glimmer of light beyond a wall blocking his path.

The wall seemed to move, and the light filtering through it danced off the stones in the passageway. Nate reached out to touch it and found it wasn't a stone wall at all. It had a coarse backing and swayed like some sort of blanket. He pulled it aside and entered a well-lit room.

Light from hundreds of candles assaulted his vision. Instead of dust and cobwebs from hundreds of years of neglect, order greeted him. Ceiling-high shelves filled with books lined two walls of the vast room. A tapestry hung over the passageway he had entered, depicting scenes of hunting dogs and wild horses, and another tapestry hung between two boarded-up windows.

A stone fireplace, large enough to roast a cow, took up the space of the remaining wall. In the center of the room was a long table, so highly polished it reflected the silver chandelier hanging from the ceiling.

"You should not have come here, my lord," Fiona said. "The killers have returned, and they are looking for you."

Chapter Sixteen

Nate felt slivers of ice run through his veins instead of warm blood. Fiona had said the killers had returned. Carl was out there all alone. And who wanted him dead? He was a nobody. "I have to help my friend, Carl."

"I no longer sense your friend, my lord. Perhaps he has left?"

That would make sense. He had told Carl to leave if he did not return in fifteen or twenty minutes. Nate paced the library like a caged animal. Physical activity had always been his salvation. It enabled him to think clearly. It was the real reason he'd picked a sport like cross-country.

"There has to be a reason Aaron was killed," he said. "No one does anything without a motive. I'm a perfect example. I always have a reason for what I do. Mostly I want to see if I can get away with it."

"You must accept it, my lord. There is evil in the world of the living and the dead," Fiona said.

She spoke so low Nate barely heard the words. Fiona's voice sounded desolate. He caught the emphasis she placed on the word "evil." It surprised him that someone who was dead could be afraid.

Nate stopped pacing. Suddenly he was curious about the ghost who had saved his life and spoke of evil as though it was a constant companion.

"How did you die?"

Fiona paused and looked distressed. "What does it matter? I am dead."

"It matters." And Nate realized that it did.

Fiona sighed. "It was a long time ago, my lord. Perhaps I want to forget."

"That much I figured out for myself," Nate answered. "Let's start with something simple. What do you remember of how you arrived in North Carolina?"

"I do not know the exact year, my lord, but it was before North Carolina became part of your United States. I do not remember much about the journey except that we were on a ship, and my father and I were afraid to leave the hold of the ship where a section of the castle had been stored. And I can see from your expression that you want to persist in your questioning. Regarding how I died, I would prefer not to speak of it."

The pain Nate heard in her voice struck through the barrier he had built over the years. He could understand the need for privacy. Nate considered himself an expert on keeping his feelings concealed.

He walked over to the fireplace. "You keep calling me 'my lord,' not that I mind," he said, smiling. "But that's not something a girl calls a guy these days."

"What should I call you?"

"My name is Nate."

As he reached the fireplace he noticed a portrait of a young woman over the mantel. The candles cast a warm glow over the entire room, but the picture had been lost in shadows until he walked closer to it.

The young woman in the portrait had flame-red hair cascading past her shoulders in fiery curls. Her eyes twinkled with an amber glow and a smile lit up her face.

"My father had the painting commissioned for my

seventeenth birthday when I was betrothed to be married. It was not a happy time. The marriage had been arranged before I was born, and I did not love the man. But not long after it was completed, I..."

"...died," Nate finished. He had sensed her presence before she spoke this time. It should have made him nervous, knowing a ghost was so close, but it didn't. He hadn't known her long, but already he considered her a friend. "How did you...I mean did someone...?"

"You are persistent."

Nate let out the breath of air he'd been holding. "I guess I am."

"What you really want to know is if I was murdered." Her voice held an edge to it as she left his side and glided across the room. "There was a ball at our castle in Edinburgh, Scotland, celebrating my betrothal. There were so many people, and the music could be heard all over the castle. My father and I argued, and I slipped away to meet someone." She paused, and there was a dreamy, almost happy expression in her eyes. "His name was Jeremy, and he and I were going to run away together. But something went terribly wrong, and he died. I do not remember what happened next, only that I realized I was dead."

He sensed she knew more than she wanted to share. He really couldn't blame her. "How can you talk so calmly about your own death?"

"I have had a long time to think about that night."

A chilling breeze whirled through the room. Candles flickered and the tapestries on the wall moved in the sudden wind. The chandelier swayed as though caught in the wind.

"Oh, no," Fiona said. "He is coming. You must run.

He does not like me talking to strangers."

"Who's coming?"

"My father. The Wolf of Nor Loch."

Nate heard panic in her voice and felt it seep into his bones. He didn't like his father much for abandoning him and his mother, but his mother had never nicknamed him anything more ominous than reckless. The Wolf of Nor Loch sounded seriously bad news.

"He never comes here. My father must not find you in the library. He killed the last person I talked to."

Nate held his breath. If he was not mistaken, she had just admitted her father killed the man she had planned to run away with. "No offense, but besides rattling a few chains and trying to scare me away, what can he do?"

"Be still," Fiona snapped, her voice rising in fear. "You must not say such things. There is a great deal my father can do. He…"

Before Fiona could finish her sentence, the flames in the fireplace died down to glowing embers before sputtering out, and the candles on the table were snuffed out, leaving trails of smoke wafting into the air. The silence was replaced by the howling of the wind.

"What was that?" he whispered, suppressing the desire to bolt for the door.

"My father."

Total darkness surrounded him, accompanied by the feeling that unfriendly eyes were watching.

"You have to leave," Fiona said. Her voice seemed so close that Nate imagined feeling her breath on his face.

"Leaving sounds like a good plan. Except I can't see a thing in the dark, and the app on my cell isn't working. And besides, I don't want to leave you."

Nate heard an object hit the floor. It was followed by a rapid succession of the same loud thuds, like a muffled Gatling gun.

"My father is in a rage. He is throwing my beautiful books off the shelves. He hopes to scare you."

"He's succeeding."

"Nate, follow close behind me."

"Follow you? How can I follow you? I can't see you."

"Do not be afraid," she said, gently taking his hand.

Her fingers were soft, feminine, and cold. Startled, he tried pulling his hand free. "You're a ghost. How is it that you can hold my hand?"

"You ask too many questions. Follow me," she said, pulling him forward. "We have to hurry."

He heard books toppling from the shelves. They whooshed through the air close to his head.

"Okay, I get the message," he said, willing the panic out of his voice.

Nate ran blindly behind Fiona, with only the pressure of her hand to guide him. A blast of freezing air hit him in the face. He staggered. The gentle pressure of Fiona's fingers pulled him forward, enabling him to regain his balance.

He sensed when the stone floor changed to carpet, but he still could not see anything but a gray blur as he ran.

Another blast of cold air and Nate saw light up ahead. It was an open doorway. As he ran through the opening, the carpet changed to a dirt floor—but where was Carl? Nate had advised him to leave, but Carl would have left a note.

Fiona stood beside him, the very image of her

portrait. No, that was not correct. She was more beautiful than her picture. "You look real. I never thought if a ghost appeared it would look so lifelike."

Fiona shrugged her shoulders. "I can only remain visible for short periods of time, and the effort drains my strength."

Nate reached out hesitantly and touched Fiona's shoulder. It was as solid as his. This was nuts. He pulled back his hand as if it had touched a flame. *What am I getting myself caught up in?*

He walked past her, heading toward the ladder. He needed to distance himself from this place. He reached for the ladder and climbed to the surface.

First one of his best friends had been hanged. Next, he was accused of murder. Of course, he hadn't been formally charged, but there were those in town who thought he might have murdered his friend. Everyone except Ruth Ann and Carl and his mother—and a ghost.

None of this came close to insanity compared with the growing attraction he felt toward Fiona. She was a ghost that didn't act or feel like she had been dead for centuries. He reached the top rung of the ladder and climbed over.

A welcome breeze of fresh air greeted him, and he started to relax. He'd get his Jeep and check on Carl and tell him that he was no closer to finding Aaron's killer than when they started. Tonight was a big dead end.

"Where are you going?"

Nate jumped, startled at the sound of Fiona's voice. "Don't do that. At least give me a little warning when you sneak up on a guy. Leave me alone."

"Why are you so angry?"

"Angry at you? I'm not. I'm angry with myself. I've

been talking to a ghost instead of looking for Aaron's killer."

Fiona reached out her hand toward Nate, her soft amber eyes brimming with tears.

Nate avoided her touch and the sorrow he saw reflected in her eyes. "Look," he said, "all my life I've been letting people down. My mother needed me when my dad left, and instead of helping her through it, I became my high school's best drop-out candidate and screw-up. I knew Aaron was mixed up in something he couldn't handle, but I didn't bother to ask if I could help."

"I can help you find your friend's killer," Fiona said.

"How can you help me? You don't even know who caused your own death, and you've had a long time to figure it out. Plus, you said you can't go beyond the school's property lines. You're stuck here."

Fiona slowly brushed a tear from her cheek. "Maybe finding out how I died isn't important anymore."

"Look, I'm sorry. I'm always putting my mouth in gear before my brain is turned on. I know you want to help. But this is something I must do on my own."

He reached out to her, but it was too late. She had vanished.

Chapter Seventeen

In class the next day, Nate had a tough time sitting still. Fiona had disappeared last night and so had Carl.

The somber thought echoed in Nate's mind as he sat in his English Lit class. He tried listening to his teacher, Mr. Bordon, preach about the benefits of reading Sherlock Holmes. Something about deductive reasoning, or was it intuition? Nate could never remember.

His eyelids felt heavy. He fought the urge to close them. He hadn't slept for more than a few hours. He kept reliving each moment he'd spent with Fiona.

After leaving the football field, he'd checked to see if Carl had gone home. His friend's mom said Carl had not come home yet, but she wasn't worried. Carl had told her he planned to be late. Nate left the message that he'd see Carl at school the next day.

Nate had driven around aimlessly and remembered getting home about three in the morning. As usual, his mom had waited up, even though she had worked late at the theater. She asked how his day was. He asked how her day was. They lied to each other, and each said they had a wonderful day. Pretty standard exchange.

There was a time, before his dad left, that she would grill him. Nate guessed she was just worn out.

"Nate Collier!" Mr. Bordon snapped, intruding into Nate's thoughts. "Care to comment on today's readings?"

"Mr. Bordon is talking about the story called *The Red-Headed League*," whispered a helpful voice behind him.

Ruth Ann was rescuing him again. He glanced over his shoulder. Today, her hair had been pulled back with a hair clip shaped like a butterfly, and she wore a bulky orange-and-pink sweater over a short skirt. She looked good.

He started to thank her for helping her when the floor rolled like waves and the pen on his desk slid toward the edge. Nate caught it before it fell. Books on the desks of students next to him dropped to the ground as the windows shuddered. A ceiling tile plummeted to the floor, missing a student by inches.

"Earthquake," a student screamed.

"We're all going to die," shouted another as the students bolted to the door.

"No one is going to die." Mr. Bordon held up his hands. "Students. Stay calm. No one panic."

Just then the bell rang, sounding shrill in Nate's ears. It wasn't the bell dismissing class, it was the emergency bell. The announcement over the intercom clicked on.

The voice of the principal blurted over the loudspeaker, "Students. This is not a drill. Vacate the school immediately."

After the first initial panic, students filed out in an orderly manner, as though practicing for a fire drill.

Nate turned around to view the back of the school. The roof of the classroom at the end of the building had collapsed and the windows had blown out. The principal used a megaphone to announce that no one had been hurt, but given the unsettling event, they were giving the students the day off while they assessed the damage.

The announcement drew a round of cheers. Good timing, Nate thought. It would give him more time to search for Carl.

Chapter Eighteen

The day after the earthquake, it was business as usual as Nate entered the school and navigated the crowded corridors. He hadn't heard from Carl and neither had Ruth Ann, which had them both worried.

They had gone through likely scenarios on reasons why Carl had ghosted them, starting with the comment that they hated the term "ghosted" on many levels.

Some of the reasons they reached as to why Carl hadn't returned their calls ranged from their friend being engaged in an online video game marathon or was someplace without cell service. What went unsaid was that neither of them believed either of those excuses. Which was why this morning he'd called the police and reported his friend missing. So far, he hadn't received a response.

Nate headed for the lockers that hugged the corridor wall as though their life depended on it. They'd once been painted purple, one of the school's colors, and then someone had the bright idea to paint them over with teal, the other school color. The result had been disastrous. The purple seeped through, resulting in a molted effect that resembled snakeskin. The PTA thought it brilliant, since they were the Mighty Pythons, and so the lockers had remained untouched.

Hinkle came up beside him. "What's the hurry?"

"What do you want?" Nate shot back over his

shoulder as he reached his locker and twirled the lock.

Even in grammar school, he and Hinkle had never been friends. The guy never did anything unless it was of direct benefit to Pete Hinkle, and it had never been beneficial for Nate and Hinkle to be friends.

"I heard you and Carl were snooping around where they found Aaron's body. What were you doing there?" Hinkle said, leaning his shoulder against a locker.

Nate wasn't surprised Hinkle had heard that he and Carl had visited the excavation site. In a school the size of Pinedale, nothing stayed secret for long.

"You're leaning on my locker," Nate said evenly. Hinkle had the reputation as the school's star football player, but Nate had earned a reputation of his own. The school's self-appointed sports god might outweigh him, but they were about the same height and everyone at school considered Nate a powder keg, just waiting for someone to light the fuse.

The urban legend stemmed from an incident that occurred the night Nate's father left. At the ripe old age of twelve, Nate had hot-wired a car and taken off after his dad with the intent of going with him or stopping him. At the time, both scenarios had warred within him. He'd ended up crashing the car into a tree, and from all accounts he'd been dead for a few seconds before he'd been revived. Near death experience number two. He guessed the third time he tempted death would be his last.

But the legend as a hothead grew over time, with the retelling, and instead of a boy trying to beg his dad not to leave, the story evolved into one where Nate was out of control and meant to do his father harm.

His friends never believed the stories. They knew

the truth, but it served Nate's purpose. Being alone suited him.

He met Hinkle's glare with one of his own.

Hinkle hesitated and then backed away from the locker. "Take it down a notch. I only want to talk."

Nate smothered a smile, concentrating on his locker combination. He filed the added information he'd learned about Hinkle away. The football hero had backed down from him too easily. Usually, it took more posturing on both their parts. That could mean either Hinkle had taken Nate's reputation to heart, or the guy wanted something and wouldn't risk ticking Nate off until he got what he came for. The latter was more likely.

Hinkle's voice sounded impatient. "You didn't answer my question. What were you and Man Mountain doing on the football field yesterday?"

"It's none of your business," Nate said, opening his locker door and tossing his English Lit book on top of a pile of textbooks and sweats.

"Carl is not in school. Just thought you might have a clue as to where he is."

Nate felt he was going to suffocate. He looked at the hallway packed with students. They were laughing and talking in a constant drone of sound. All of them sucking the oxygen out of the air.

Reluctantly, Nate knew Hinkle was right. The fact that Carl hadn't contacted him was not good.

"Hey, Ruth Ann," Hinkle shouted. "Watch where you're going."

The threatening sound of Hinkle's voice jarred Nate. It was a new low, even for the football star. Ruth Ann cringed under Hinkle's glare.

It was a common occurrence. Hinkle enjoyed

finding vulnerable victims for his verbal and physical assaults. But today was different. Today Hinkle had deliberately chosen Ruth Ann because he knew she and Nate were friends.

"Leave her alone," Nate said, taking the few steps necessary to place himself between Hinkle and Ruth Ann.

"This in none of your business," Hinkle said.

Nate shoved Hinkle against the locker, drawing the attention of students. "I'm making it my business."

"No need to get mad," Hinkle said. "You really do have a temper. I dare you to try and hit me with all these witnesses present. You'd get suspended for life."

Nate knew it wouldn't be for life, but he couldn't risk suspension when he had to be on school grounds if he had any hope of solving Aaron's murder and Carl's disappearance.

Nate drew back as Hinkle smirked and swaggered off toward class with his hands in his pockets, whistling off key.

Ruth Ann frowned in Hinkle's direction. "That knuckle dragger provoked you deliberately. He knew you would stick up for me. By third period the school will say you have an out-of-control temper."

"They're not wrong."

Chapter Nineteen

Ruth Ann had left for class, leaving Nate by the locker bay. She had been right. It would be all over school about him shoving Hinkle against a locker. It was a short hop, a skip, and a jump before they all started remembering the fight he and Aaron had had.

He slammed his locker shut and kicked it for good measure. "Carl, where are you?" The dark thoughts returned. He felt his emotions were on a roller coaster ride.

He traced over the last twenty-four hours. He hadn't seen Carl since he'd been at the MacGregor ruin, or what students had started referring to as the Haunted Castle. Why had he left Carl alone?

"How could I be so stupid?" Carl would never have left, even though Nate had told him to. He was that kind of a guy. Why hadn't he checked back with Carl's mom? Maybe his friend had never made it home.

The school's bell announcing the next class sliced through Nate's thoughts. Now would be a good time to slip out of school and search for Carl. Between periods was the best time, he had discovered, or when you were returning from or going to a school assembly. It was that sweet spot, that in-between time when teachers rarely paid attention.

Someone touched his shoulder.

He whirled around, expecting trouble.

"Hey, there, slow down," said the man who'd put his hand on Nate's shoulder and then quickly removed it. "I'm not looking for a fight, just Nate Collier. Remember me? I'm Counselor Williams. I was introduced at the assembly as the new substitute school counselor when Counselor Copeland took a leave of absence."

Counselor Williams was shorter than Nate, shaved head, broader in the shoulder, and light gray eyes. He had broken up the fight Nate had had with Aaron. That event seemed light-years ago instead of days.

Nate shook Williams' hand, recognizing the type: high energy, grand expectations, and the type who would blame himself if he couldn't turn everyone away from the dark side.

"Your mother," Counselor Williams began, "asked me if I would talk to you about Aaron."

Direct approach. Usually, the counselors he'd seen in the past spent a half an hour or more trying to bond with him over current bands or musicians. The worst was when they lied to his face about how they also liked to run long distances. But even if Counselor Williams did have a direct, honest approach, Nate didn't have the time. He had to find Carl.

Nate shook his head slowly. "I must get to class. Maybe some other time."

"I've already let your teacher know you won't be in class this period. My office is down the hall. Why don't we start right now?"

So much for skipping school, Nate thought as he followed Williams toward his office. Nate considered being rude to the guy but knew it would upset his mom. She was trying to help him. She didn't know how to talk to him, so she was reaching out for help. It wasn't her fault. It was just that when it came to communication or life goals they lived on different planets. She wanted him to be a success. Nate just wanted to survive.

"Here we are," Counselor Williams said, stopping at a door with the word "Counselor" etched in the glass. "It's still a little disorganized," he said, opening the door and pushing boxes out of the way.

A little disorganized would have been an improvement. Nate smiled to himself. The counselor's office was in worse shape than his bedroom.

Counselor Williams pointed to a chair as he cleared papers off the seat. "Why don't you sit down, and we can start."

Nate did as he was told and took the time to look around the room. All the available space on chairs, shelves, window ledges and the floor was strewn with a haphazard assortment of notebooks and file folders. In contrast, the walls displayed pictures of mountain vistas and rock climbers.

Nate rose from the chair to take a better look at the photos. "This is you," he said pointing to a man climbing up a sheer cliff.

Counselor Williams sat down behind a desk where books competed for space with a laptop computer. "Climbing is what I do to relax. I can't think about my problems when I'm fighting for a toehold in solid rock."

"I run," Nate said, sitting back down in the chair.

Counselor Williams nodded, reaching for a short length of rope on his desk. He began twisting it into knots. "I'd be glad to take you out sometime. 'Course you'd have to learn to tie your own knots. Never trust anyone to do it for you is my motto. It's a rule of the mountain that you're responsible for your own gear."

"Sounds fair."

"A good place for you to start would be on Linville Gorge or Hawksbill Mountain."

Nate knew the places Williams mentioned. His father had talked about climbing there more than once but they'd never gotten around to it. "Not interested."

"Too bad." Counselor Williams tossed the rope to the side. "Do you believe in ghosts? You're not the first person in this school to claim to see one. I heard you mentioned you'd seen one the night Aaron was murdered."

The counselor's question seemed to be rehearsed, and Nate couldn't shake the feeling that he knew him. One thing was certain. The counselor had an agenda. Nate just wasn't sure what it was. "That's the story I told the police."

"You'd rather not talk about it. We'll talk about something else. I've been meaning to ask about your running. I used to run in high school, mostly short distances, but enough to appreciate the sport and recognize talent. You earned your nickname, Road Warrior. You own whatever race you're in. I have a question, though. If Aaron was in the race, you'd always pull up right before the finish line. Why did you always let him win?"

His mother accused him of switching topics in the middle of a sentence, and the new counselor had the same annoying habit. Nate used it to avoid a topic. He sensed that Counselor Williams used it to throw a person off guard. Nate gripped the armrests. "Our time is up."

Counselor Williams held up his hand and leaned forward. "Hold on. Your secret is safe with me. You had your reasons. I know the sport and I've seen you run. You're the best cross-country runner to come along in the last ten to fifteen years. Colleges would have been knocking down your door, but you chose to let your friend shine and gobble up all the glory. Perhaps you felt he needed it more. Again, not my business."

"You're right. It's none of your business." Nate leaned back in his chair, trying to distance himself from Counselor Williams. "It was more important to Aaron to win. He really wanted to go to college, but his parents couldn't afford more than a community college. He figured the only way to get there was with a scholarship. Aaron had good grades, so it would have happened for him."

"We'll talk about your grades later. Did Aaron know you were letting him win?"

"Probably, but we never talked about it. Carl knew and understood my reasons."

"It must have bothered you, knowing Aaron was getting all the attention."

Was the counselor working with the police? The counseling session sounded more like an interrogation.

"Why should it have bothered me? My grades are barely above average, so college was out for me."

"What about Cindy Fremont?"

Nate stood up so abruptly his chair toppled over. "You don't understand anything."

Counselor Williams steepled his hands. "Maybe I don't or maybe I do. I can understand how a kid could box himself into a corner. In the beginning, being the first one to cross the finish line hadn't mattered. You had nothing to gain. Then along came Cindy. Did you ever wonder whether, if you had been the one setting the records, she would have chosen you instead of Aaron? Of course, by that time you couldn't change things. You were too locked into this fantasy where Aaron was faster. Still, if Aaron was no longer in the picture…"

"Are you accusing me of murdering Aaron? He was my best friend! I'm out of here."

Nate half expected Counselor Williams to stop him. Once outside the counselor's office, he glanced back through the window. The counselor was dialing his cell. It was either Nate's mother or the police. The way his luck ran, it was the police.

The bell had rung and there was a class change in progress. A good time to skip school.

Nate had to find Carl.

Chapter Twenty

Nate drove slowly up the driveway to Carl's two-toned beige split-entry home. He had to find out why his friend wasn't in school today. Nate hoped one of the scenarios he and Ruth had thought about for the reason Carl was AWOL was true and Carl would say he had been caught up in a marathon online game and lost track of time.

He parked his Jeep, hoping Carl was sick and would greet him at the door. Maybe he had the flu. No, the guy was the healthiest person at school. He never got sick. Maybe he wanted to avoid a test? Nate ruled that out as well. Skipping classes was not Carl's way. He loved school and met his problems head on.

Frustrated, Nate hit the steering wheel with the palm of his hand. Stop procrastinating! It was time to face why Carl was absent, regardless of the outcome.

Nate exited the Jeep and dragged his feet as he walked the short distance to the front porch. A wreath of plastic flowers in fall colors hung on the front door. When Nate was younger, he wished his mother was more like Carl's. Carl's mother decorated the house and baked for every season and holiday. He wasn't sure how it happened, but one day he woke up and realized he was just grateful he had a mother who loved him, unconditionally.

If Carl wasn't sick or skipping school, the other

alternative scared the life out of him. Had he been kidnapped? Or worse. His hands were sweaty as he knocked on the front door with enough force that a gold leaf was jangled to the ground.

Carl's mother, Sarah Wilson, opened the door. Tall, slender, with short carrot-red hair the same shade as her son's, she gave a quick nod toward Nate. Normally her face broke into smiles when she saw him. Today she was acting like it was the end of the world. Not a good sign.

Nate picked up the plastic leaf that had fallen and handed it to Mrs. Wilson. "I just came to see how Carl was doing, Mrs. Wilson."

"I was expecting you." She reached for the leaf he handed her, fingering it as she motioned for him to enter and follow her down a hallway and into the living room.

She had dodged his question regarding Carl and, instead of directing him to Carl's bedroom or the kitchen, she was leading him to their living room. Nate could count on the one hand the number of times he'd been in Carl's living room. Four times had been to celebrate a birthday and the last time was for Carl's father's wake.

The smell of chocolate wafted in the air. If Nate was to venture a guess, Carl's mother was baking her famous chocolate-and-peanut-butter brownies. Except she rarely baked during the week. Her habit was to bake on the weekend so Carl would be home in time to get one straight out of the oven.

He followed her into the living room, which hadn't changed since he'd been here three years ago. The colors were in the shades of the sand dunes he'd seen on a National Geographic documentary, and they reminded him of a desert. The sofa was a dusty brown and matched the twin overstuffed chairs by the window. The accent pillows were yellow, red, and copper, and a handmade patch quilt was slung over the arm of the sofa. The colors were restful in stark contrast to how he felt.

"Well, we meet again," a man in a navy suit said, as he emerged from the far corner of the room and held out his hand.

"Detective Henshaw," Nate said, recognized him from Aaron's funeral. Shaking the offered hand automatically, Nate looked from Mrs. Wilson to the detective. Nate had been right to worry about his friend.

"Detective Henshaw," Mrs. Wilson said, "is a friend of Aaron's family. I think he was most kind to come all the way from Los Angeles to help with the case. Don't you think so, Nate?"

Nate nodded in response to her question. Well, that explained why he hadn't seen Henshaw before, and why the man was so persistent.

"Aaron used to write me about you," Henshaw said. "I have the advantage. I know more about you than you do about me. Of course, that's the ideal position a detective likes to have. Don't you agree?"

The only thing Nate agreed upon was that silence would be his best tactic, especially until he could figure out what this detective was really fishing for. He remembered Aaron talking about his mom having a brother that was a cop, but Aaron had not elaborated. Aaron had earned his reputation as a man of few words.

"Aaron wasn't kidding when he said you were short on conversation. Did school get out a little early today? Don't bother answering. I already know you skipped class."

Henshaw reached into his jacket and drew out a pad and pencil. Old school. Most detectives used an iPad or their cell to take notes. For some reason, using pen and paper was more intimidating. Maybe that's why he did it.

"I skipped because I was worried about Carl."

"Is that so. Mrs. Wilson, would you mind getting me a cup of that coffee you offered earlier? And something smells delicious."

"I'm baking brownies. But they aren't ready yet. I'll put on a pot of coffee. Nate, do you want anything?"

"No, thank you. I'm fine." The detective obviously wanted to ask him questions without Carl's mother present.

"Why don't you sit down?" Henshaw said as he pointed toward the chair closest to the sofa.

Nate obeyed the order. He was taking a lot of orders these days. In some ways it was easier.

"When was the last time you saw Carl Wilson?"

Nate took an even breath. "It was the evening of the funeral."

The detective looked up from his notepad. "Was that the first or second time you went to the school?"

Had Henshaw been following him? Nate rubbed his sweaty palms on his jeans.

"If you know so much, why are you asking me questions?"

"Okay, so that's how you want to play this. You and Carl were seen heading over to the football field. I figure the two of you were planning to do a little detective work on your own in the excavation tunnels. Maybe look for clues or cover up your tracks. This is not my jurisdiction, but it's personal. Aaron was my nephew, remember."

"There is a track that runs around the football field. We went there to run." Lying was getting easier. Was that how it had been with his dad? Once he started lying, he couldn't stop?

"You weren't dressed for running," the detective said.

"We always have spare running gear in the trunk." Nated waited as the detective scribbled notes on his pad.

"You know," Henshaw said, "sometimes amateur detectives stumble onto clues overlooked by the police. Are you sure you and Carl didn't find something that could be helpful?"

"I told you. We just went for a run."

Nate looked with renewed interest at the detective. Usually, he could figure out where any line of questioning was leading. It was a skill he had developed from years in the hot seat in the principal's office. "Why do you want to know whether or not Carl and I looked for missed evidence?"

"Just curious," Henshaw said as he resumed his scribbling.

If it was one thing Nate had learned, it was that adults, especially ones who were interrogating him, never asked questions merely for curiosity's sake. It was time he ended this interrogation. If Carl wasn't home, where was he? It wasn't like Carl not to contact him.

"If you don't have any more questions, I should get back to school," Nate said, standing.

Henshaw stood up as well and put his pen and notebook back in his jacket pocket. "I'm sure the police here have advised you not to leave town."

"Is someone leaving?" Mrs. Wilson said as she returned with the coffee.

"I have to leave, Mrs. Wilson," said Nate.

"I should get going too," Henshaw said. "Mrs.

Wilson, it's been a pleasure."

Carl's mother nodded and showed the detective to the door. Henshaw handed Mrs. Wilson his card. "I'm sticking around town for a few more days. Be sure to let me know if Carl returns or contacts you."

Mrs. Wilson reached for the card and gave Henshaw a nod. "Thank you for coming, Detective."

"You coming?" Henshaw said to Nate.

"Nate's staying with me for a while longer," Mrs. Wilson answered abruptly.

"Very well." Henshaw tipped his head in a goodbye and headed to a nondescript tan rental car parked along the sidewalk.

Mrs. Wilson waited until Henshaw drove out of the neighborhood before she shut the door.

"I don't trust that man. I'd never met him before the funeral. But Carl trusts you and so do I. If anyone can find Carl, it's you."

"Don't worry, Mrs. Wilson, Carl can take care of himself."

"He can if it's just the living he has to worry about." Her eyes were bright with the look of fear. "But what if it's true?"

"What are you talking about?"

"There are people in town who say it's the ghost that killed Aaron. The one that appeared soon after they dug up the football field. Wait here. I have something for you."

Carl's mother grew more fearful as each second ticked by. It was obvious to him that she was worried. He was as well. Of course, having a detective interrogating your son's friends in your own home wasn't helping. He needed to distract her from the supernatural.

When she returned, she held out a paper sack. "Brownies, fresh from the oven."

"I thought everyone in town believed I was the prime suspect. Are you telling me I'm off the hook?"

"Don't you be joking about something this serious." Mrs. Wilson handed Nate the bag of brownies and shoved him out the door. "Now don't forget. Take care of Carl. He trusts you to do the right thing. And don't shove the brownie into your mouth and eat it in one bite. Take your time. I made them especially for you."

It wasn't until Nate was heading away from Carl's house in his Jeep that the thought hit him. Henshaw had asked him if he and Carl had done any detective work when he and Carl were in the excavated underground tunnels. He searched his memory for anything he might have said about that night. He had not mentioned what he and Carl had been doing. He glanced in his rearview mirror and thought he saw a car following him. He was becoming as paranoid as Mrs. Wilson.

He slowed down, then stopped at the stop sign, and when he glanced in the rearview mirror, the street was deserted.

Nate gripped the steering wheel. His thoughts flew to Fiona and her gentle smile. He had never believed in ghosts or goblins until he met her. Now his mind was conjuring up imagined dangers at every turn. An uneasiness took hold of him as he headed toward town. He had to find Carl. And he wanted to see Fiona again. He couldn't shake the feeling that Fiona—and her father—were connected to Aaron's death.

He reached over and grabbed one of Mrs. Wilson's brownies. Nate hadn't had time for breakfast and the smell was a sudden reminder. Nate bit into the brownie and tasted paper.

"What the…"

He pulled over to the side of the road and unfolded the paper from the brownie. The paper was written in Carl's handwriting. His friend's writing was so small that a magnifying glass was needed to read it. Carl's teachers had insisted he type his papers because they had given up trying to read the small print. Nate's eyesight was eagle-eye good.

Nate,

If you're reading this, it means I'm in hiding.

Look in our secret locker. Tell no one what you found.

Don't search for me. I'll find you.

C

Chapter Twenty-One

Carl was alive.

Nate's heart raced as though he had finished a marathon. He hadn't realized how worried he was for his friend until reading that note. "Where are you, Carl? You don't want me to search for you. Like hell, I won't."

But first things first. Carl wanted him to find something in their secret locker, the one for which no one except he, Carl, and Aaron, knew the combination. Was there a clue to where Carl was hiding?

The world was upside down. That was the only way Nate could explain it. Nate started his Jeep. It rumbled to life. The news in the note was the best he'd received in days. Carl was alive. He'd no doubt been at his home and instructed his mom to put the note in her brownies. But why hadn't she just told Nate? Why all the secrecy? What was Carl's mother afraid of? And what had spooked Carl so badly that he had gone into hiding?

Nate felt helpless, and that was a dark place. He had not been able to prevent his father from leaving, and he didn't know how to help his mother climb out of the deep depression that held her prisoner. Then there was Aaron…and Carl.

The one bright spot was that Ruth Ann was solid. Nothing bothered her.

He pushed down the weight in his chest and blinked to clear his vision as he drove down the street toward school and rolled to a stop at a stoplight. Traffic was heavy. People driving to or from someplace. On the surface they looked like mindless ants. But he knew better. Every one of them carried a weight on their shoulders. Just some people hid the earth-crushing enormity of it better than others.

Now, all Nate had to do was sneak back into school. That was a bit more challenging than skipping. Students had the option of eating lunch off campus, but because the school's security was tight these days since Aaron's murder, there would have been a record of him leaving for the lunch break, so it would be tricky to sneak back into school—but not impossible. He'd done it before. It all boiled down to the story.

The simpler the better. Too many details tripped you up. That's where most students failed. That, and the number of people involved. The more people who participated, the more chances someone would forget the story and go off script.

It was the end of the lunch break and students would be returning from town. All he needed to do was stroll, all casual-like, back into school as though he had stepped out for a burger and fries. His story was easy, with a built-in excuse. It was common knowledge that he, Carl, and Aaron, rarely left for lunch. He, because he couldn't afford it, and Aaron and Carl because they wanted to keep him company. And good weather or bad, they ate their lunches on the football bleachers.

If confronted, he would say that with Aaron dead, and Carl missing, he couldn't face eating alone, and went into town for lunch or to spend time with his mother. He'd apologize that, with everything going on, he must have forgotten to check out of school. Not as simple an explanation as he would have liked. Too many moving parts, and if the school checked with his mother, she wouldn't lie for him.

He parked his Jeep in the junior lot and walked toward the school's entrance. He'd timed it perfectly. Half the students were returning, laughing, flirting, and posing for pictures as though Aaron wasn't dead, Carl wasn't missing, and a murderer wasn't on the loose. He felt like screaming.

Ruth Ann ran over to him.

"What are you doing here?" he said.

"Hello to you too, grumpy face. And keep your voice down," she warned, steering him from the sidewalk to a canopy of trees on the school's lawn. "I'm saving you from detention or worse. Everyone thinks you skipped school."

"And they would be right. I've got it covered."

"If you're going to use the alibi that you couldn't bear having lunch by yourself and that's the reason you went into town, you're going to have to come up with a better story."

"Okay, so you're right about the story. You a mind reader now?"

"Only when it comes to you. When I realized you had skipped, I told the principal that I asked you to go to my house and retrieve the signed permission slip I left on the kitchen counter."

"One major flaw. Why wouldn't your mother arrange a way to get this to you?"

The smile in her eyes dimmed for a split second as her mouth quivered into a smile.

"I'm sure she would have, but she and my dad are still on a business trip in New York. They are the lead prosecutors in a difficult insurance scam case and won't return until next week."

"That's terrible." And he wasn't referring to her parents' difficult case. He was referring to her parents being gone all the time. Maybe she wasn't as solid as he thought. Maybe she was simply better at hiding how she felt than he was.

She glanced over her shoulder. "I'm sure they'll win the case. They always do."

"I wasn't talking about the stupid case. How are you doing?"

She kept her focus on a couple walking hand in hand toward the school's entrance. "I'm fine. Really. I like it better when they're gone."

"Okay. If you say so. Change of subject. You know they're going to ask where's your car and why didn't you scan the permission slip, and couldn't your parents sign and send the permission form in to the office?"

She shrugged, grinning. "Great questions, counselor. I have that covered. For some reason my car won't start, and my parents can't be reached."

"Lame. But the principal and her minions believed you because, well, you are you."

She wiggled her eyebrows. "I also cried."

Windows from the school's library shattered. Smoke and flames billowed out through the cracks, breaking the glass. A student on the sidewalk nearest Nate screamed, "Fire!" More students joined in, and some punched into their cells to dial 911, while others went racing away from the school.

The fire alarm blared over the loudspeakers as students raced from the building in a continuing wave of panic.

Nate reached for Ruth Ann around her waist and spun her out of the way and under the shelter of a large oak tree as students poured out of the school. He put his hands on her shoulders. "Run," he shouted over the chaos.

As soon as she reached the parking lot, he turned and jogged toward the school.

He didn't get far. He was met with a wall of students and one incredibly angry counselor—Williams.

"Hey, where do you think you're going?"

"I want to help."

"The janitor is checking the building, and the fire department will be here soon. Williams tugged Nate away from the building and toward the parking lot. "You'll only get in their way," he said over the roar of the student's screams and the blare of the oncoming fire truck sirens.

"Do you know who started the fire?" Nate asked.

"Not a clue. A real tragedy. though. I caught a glimpse of the library when I was helping students exit the building. Likely all the books are destroyed, but they can be replaced. We stored the school's archives in the library, and those records are irreplaceable."

Chapter Twenty-Two

Several hours later the fire department had determined that the school was safe for the students who wanted to retrieve belongings from their lockers before going home. Still no clue as to how the fire had started, but that wasn't his problem. If it hadn't been for the message Nate had received from Carl, Nate would have bailed, like two-thirds of the student body.

No one seemed to think it was odd that there had been a murder, an earthquake, and a fire in less than a week. Adding to the trifecta was that Carl was missing.

Nate headed back inside to check out the contents of the secret locker he shared with Aaron and Carl. The acrid smell of smoke clung to the hallways, and a fine sheen of water from the fire hoses coated the floors. It would take days to clean up this mess. He felt sorry for Hank and the other custodians. It was a thankless job.

"Looks like I'm not the only one who couldn't leave Pinedale High."

Nate turned to see Hinkle strolling toward him. Hinkle was acting like they were best buds. "I didn't have any place better to go."

"I hear ya. I hadn't planned on coming back, but Coach Riley ambushed me in the parking lot. He all but ordered me to track you down. He was in this purple rage and asked if I knew where you were, as though I was your keeper. He calmed down long enough to ask me to persuade you to join the football team. Riley thinks anyone with your speed should play football, not run in circles around a track."

"I'm not interested."

"Yeah, I told him you'd say that, but Coach Riley was acting all jittery and twitchy. He threatened to pull me from the starting line up if I didn't relay his message, so here I am in my new role as a messenger."

"Message received."

Hinkle shoved his hands in his pockets. "All kidding aside, we could use a guy with your speed on the team. Just saying. We should all stick together. You know—us against the teachers, administrators, and coaches."

"Right, like a brotherhood of dumb jocks."

"Exactly," Hinkle said. "Aaron never fully understood. But I knew you would."

Nate realized Hinkle had taken his comment seriously when he had meant it as a slam. Sometimes the guy acted as dumb as rocks, yet he had been on the honor roll since sophomore year. It was rumored that, for the right price, a student could buy any test for any class. Nate had never paid any attention to the rumors because ninety-nine percent of school rumors were bogus.

"Well, take care," Hinkle said as he slapped Nate on the shoulder. "Oh, by the way. Didn't you share a locker with Aaron?"

"Carl and I share a locker. Aaron didn't have a locker partner. Why do you ask?"

"No reason. Just wanted to know if all his things were cleaned out and given to his mom, that's all. See you in class tomorrow."

Nate watched as Hinkle proceeded toward the school's exit. "What was that all about?" Nate said aloud. He rubbed the back of his neck. This day had been strange from the beginning. The sooner he left the school the better. His thoughts drifted to Carl. Maybe he had found a clue to Aaron's killer after all and somehow slipped it into their locker.

He punched in the combination, but before he could open it, he was interrupted.

"I was looking for you," Counselor Williams said.

"You found me. Any special reason?" Nate had never had this many people hovering around him asking questions before, unless you counted the time he had been suspected of stealing the rival school's banner.

"It's about Aaron's locker. Aaron's parents were looking for an envelope they believed Aaron had left in his locker. It's important."

Nate leaned against the bank of lockers, his uneasiness returning with a vengeance. Aaron didn't have "parents." His father had died when he was four or five. Aaron's mom was a sales representative for a line of handmade gifts and spent most of her time on the road. When she did appear, it was often with some new boyfriend she'd refer to as Aaron's dad. The relationship never lasted long, and as a result, Aaron spent most of his time at either Nate's or Carl's house.

Nate willed his voice to remain calm. "Aaron and I weren't locker partners."

"True, but we thought Aaron might have said something to you about an envelope. His locker was clean, orderly, and empty, except for sweat pants, a few books, and track shoes.

A chill chased up Nate's spine. The inside of Aaron's locker had always been jammed with everything from stale sandwiches to old ticket stubs and random pieces of paper. Nate and Carl joked that their friend was a hoarder in need of intervention. No way would Aaron's locker have contained only a few books and neatly stacked shoes. It would have been a disaster zone. Something didn't fit.

This whole conversation was getting stranger by the second. Nate took a deep calming breath. Maybe he'd heard the counselor wrong. Maybe the guy had only said one parent and maybe Nate was just being paranoid. Then again, being paranoid was a good thing.

"I don't know anything about an envelope."

The counselor eyed Nate. "Do you mind if I check your locker?"

An urgent-sounding voice interrupted the counselor's question.

"Counselor Williams," a woman shouted, "you have to come at once."

Nate and the counselor turned in unison to see the school secretary running toward them. Mrs. Cherry was as wide as she was tall and could have retired years ago. She was a woman who held the belief that the welfare of all the students at Pinedale High were her responsibility. There wasn't a child she didn't like, and consequently she was well loved.

"Counselor Williams," she said as she came to an abrupt halt. "We have an emergency. You must come at once. Someone has been hurt."

"Please calm down," the counselor said. "Catch your breath and tell me what has happened."

"There's been a fight," she said between gulps of air. "It looks serious. I think one of the boys may have had a knife. They are in the clinic with the nurse. But they are still very angry. We need your help."

"What about the principal?"

"She's out of the building. A meeting in town."

The counselor turned toward Nate, a worried look on his face. "You stay right here. It's important that I talk with you. This shouldn't take long." He shoved a leaflet into Nate's hands.

Nate watched as the counselor followed Mrs. Cherry, then glanced at the flyer. It advertised a memorial party for Aaron on the night of the lunar eclipse. It was like the one Ruth Ann had given him. He stuck the flyer into his pants pocket. The memorial was a positive idea. He wasn't sure he'd attend. Parties weren't his thing.

Nate turned back to the job of opening his locker, then paused. His curiosity at what Carl could have meant in the note stuffed in the brownie had increased with the counselor's interrogation over a missing envelope.

Nate pulled open the locker he shared with Carl. They had divided the space and installed a shelf so they could keep their things separate. They had accused Aaron of being a hoarder and Aaron accused them of being OCD. They shared a laugh, a pizza, and called a truce.

Carl had said to look in the locker. But nothing was out of place, and nothing had been added.

Nate straightened as the thought stuck him. Of course. Carl's note told him to look in their secret locker.

He walked toward the end of the locker bay to the locker that had never been assigned because of the rumor that it was haunted. The story went that decades ago a student had been stuffed inside and died. Nate and his friends didn't believe the rumor, but it served their purpose. They liked having a secret locker no one knew about.

Carl, the techy of their group, had hacked the lock and changed the combination.

Nate's fingers felt cold and stiff as he worked the combination. He had to will his fingers to comply as he repeated the numbers in his mind. What would he find? When the final digit clicked, a signal that the right numbers had been used, he paused. He pulled the door open and looked inside.

Exactly as the locker he shared with Carl, nothing seemed out of place. On the floor of the locker was a pad of paper and pens stuffed in a mug with the school's Python logo. All normal stuff. If they wanted to pass each other messages, they'd use this locker, and felt like junior spies or members of a secret organization.

The hair on the back of his neck bristled. He glanced over his shoulder, feeling as though he was being watched. Other than shadows, the hallway was deserted. He laughed nervously. He was being paranoid again.

He refocused on the locker, searching for anything out of place.

A brown manila envelope peeked out from the corner of the pad of paper. He swallowed and slipped it out slowly. There was the number thirty-three written in the bottom right-hand corner. Did it refer to the number of pages inside? But how did the envelope get here? Had Carl placed it in the locker, or had Aaron put it there before he died? Was it what Aaron had been looking for?

He unfastened the clasp. It was jammed with papers. Nate thumbed through them slowly. There were answer sheets for tests for all the upper-level classes at Pinedale High. At the top of each score sheet, the words "Teacher's Copy" were printed. If these score sheets had been found in Aaron's locker, it would have been assumed that Aaron had illegally acquired the tests and he would have been expelled. Was Aaron using the answers to cheat on tests? Nate shook his head. Aaron wasn't a cheater. It was more likely that Aaron had found the answer sheets and was going to turn them in. Was that why he was murdered? But how was Carl involved?

Then an official-looking document caught his attention. At first it looked like papers from a history or political science class. There were references to how land was given to settlers before and after the American Revolution. The last page suggested there had been an ownership dispute over lands now occupied by Pinedale High School, Pinedale Cemetery Hill, and Raven Lake that had never been resolved. There was also a mention of mineral rights.

Nate ran his hand nervously through his hair. None of this made any sense. Aaron would never have cheated on a test. He didn't have to. Aaron got uptight if he missed an assignment. And why would he have stuffed documents regarding a land dispute in with the test scores?

"What are you trying to tell me, Carl?"

Chapter Twenty-Three

The next morning, the ebony night relinquished its hold as the sun awoke and splashed shades of yellows, oranges, and flame reds across the horizon. *Red sky at night, sailors delight. Red sky in the morning, sailors take warning.* But it was more than the blood-red sky that had Nate's nerves on edge. The air felt charged with an electrical current.

The familiar refrain kicked around in his head as he parked his Jeep and snagged his gym bag and backpack from the back seat. He shrugged, locking his Jeep. His father's favorite saying had less impact when every day lately had felt like danger was lurking behind every corner.

Aaron had told him through Fiona that he shouldn't trust anyone. That was the reason Nate intended to keep the envelope with him at all times.

His backpack slung over his shoulder and his gym bag in hand, Nate jogged the football field's end zone, past players who were positioned on the line of scrimmage for a practice game. Their dedication was admirable and lifted his spirits. At this hour in the morning most students were either still asleep or just rolling out of bed. But rain or shine, at the request of the head coach, the junior and varsity players practiced together. The head coach believed it boosted team spirit.

Carl had texted him this morning that he was back

in school and that he had been elevated to first string and that Assistant Coach Riley had suggested he play tight end instead of offensive lineman. Nate was happy for his friend. It was about time the coaches realized how talented he was. Nate should have felt excited for Carl, but all he felt was a deep sense of foreboding. He had received nothing from Carl over the last few days except a note in a brownie and a cryptic text. That was not like Carl.

All the players on the field reminded Nate of coiled springs. Hinkle was no exception. Unlike his usual calm demeanor, he paced like a caged animal and barked at anyone foolish enough to come within earshot.

He took his position as quarterback, waiting for the snap. The head coach was on the sidelines talking to a few of the teachers who helped him with coaching. Some, like the head coach, had been former Pinedale football players. Everyone on the sidelines seemed agitated.

Nate adjusted his backpack over his shoulder. The change in weather must be affecting everyone. At least he hoped that was all it was. He couldn't shake the feeling that something was about to happen.

Nate headed toward the gym for early morning training before school began. He was looking forward to an hour of mindless running to clear his head. It wouldn't even matter if he ran around the track a few dozen times or more instead of over the trails in the woods.

The sounds of locker doors slamming and the hum of conversation and random bursts of laughter greeted him as he entered the locker room to change into his running gear.

"Assistant Coach Riley wants to see you," Derek

said, tossing his gym bag into his locker and closing the door. Derek was tall and lean and ran the one hundred and two hundred meters race. "My guess is the coach is going to try and persuade you to play football. You've got the size and the speed for it." Derek cuffed Nate on the shoulder and laughed. "I know you're not interested, but you screwed up, my friend, when you were joking around and beat our top sprinter in the hurdles at practice."

Nate opened his locker. Riley was persistent, he'd give him that. "Yeah, that was a lapse in judgment, for sure. Is Coach Riley in his office? I didn't see him on the field."

Derek nodded. "I didn't see him myself. Carl passed me a note to give to you on his way to practice. The coach is waiting for you. See you on the track."

Nate nodded, setting his gym bag on the bench seat in the locker room, then headed toward Riley's office, located on the perimeter of the basketball court. A half dozen students were playing a game of pickup basketball and nodded to Nate as he passed.

He skirted the court and headed to the bank of five offices on the opposite side of the gym. Metal blinds were drawn over the office windows, and plaques identified the school's coaches. He slowed his pace, not looking forward to the conversation. Coach Riley wouldn't like his answer.

This must be the day for elevating a person's athletic profile. First Carl was called up to varsity, and now, if Nate suspected Coach Riley's intentions correctly, Nate would be next. Both the head coach and the assistant had suggested Nate might make a good wide receiver, running back or cornerback. That would mean working with a team. Relying on others had never been his strong suit. Too much opportunity for disappointment.

He liked the challenge and freedom of individual sports. At least that was the story he spun when he was asked. The truth was harder to explain, even to himself. Except for relays, it was up to him to win. It was on his shoulders. The only exception had been if Aaron was in the race. Pulling back a little seemed like a justifiable solution for a friend. Now that Aaron was gone, he wasn't sure what he would do.

He knocked on the assistant's door. "Coach Riley? It's Nate Collier. Derek said you wanted to see me."

What sounded like a chair being tipped over and a muffled groan seeped through the door. "Come in." Riley's voice was thick, brusque, and robotic sounding when it usually was warm and welcoming.

Coach Riley taught math and was one of the school's favorite coaches. He rarely gave homework and didn't believe in pop quizzes. The other teachers called him too easy, but Riley had another philosophy. The story had been that he had struggled himself, but a teacher had helped him succeed and he wanted to do the same. His positive attitude rubbed off on his students and he followed that up by offering a free tutoring class in the library before and after school. Nate wondered what the coach would do now that the library was under repair after the fire.

Nate turned the doorknob and eased the door open a fraction of an inch. "Coach Riley? Are you in here?" No answer but the smell of sulfur mixed with smoke filled the air. Had Coach Riley started smoking again?

He opened the door wider.

The usually orderly office looked as though it had

been hit by a hurricane. Papers and folders were strewn over the desk and floor, and filing cabinet doors hung open as though someone had been looking for something.

Coach Riley stood with his back to Nate, his shoulders rounded as he faced a wall of framed photos. There were pictures of Riley when he played football at Pinedale and in college, a framed college diploma, and coaching and teaching certificates. In the center was a large black-and-white photo of Pinedale High School in the nineteen fifties.

He traced his finger over a photo of one of the teachers in the black-and-white picture.

Nate stepped over a pile of papers and schooled his voice against sounding as worried as he felt. Riley was acting strange. "Are you okay, Coach?"

Riley turned his head over his shoulder toward Nate. His face was swollen and looked like the shade of a cooked lobster. "Not really."

"What happened to you?"

"I'm sorry, Nate." Coach Riley gasped for breath as though he couldn't get enough air into his lungs. "I didn't mean to do it." Coach Riley let out a strangled moan and collapsed like a rag doll.

Nate raced over to the coach and caught him in his arms. The momentum drove them both to the floor. The stench of burned hair and flesh swept over him. Bile rose to his throat. Coach Riley's face was blood red, disfigured, and burned beyond recognition. "Hang on. I'll get help." Nate reached for his cell to dial 911.

"No time," Coach Riley said, grabbing Nate's arm. "Just listen. It made me kill Aaron. I was not myself. You have to believe me. I'm so sorry…I…" He gasped, struggling to breathe. Nate's thoughts raced, trying to process. Coach Riley had confessed to murdering Aaron. No, that wasn't it exactly. He'd said he wasn't himself and that someone had made him kill.

Coach Riley screamed; his eyes clouded in pain. "It's looking for something. The documents weren't in the library, and it got very angry. You must stop it." His grip on Nate's arm tightened as his fingers dug into Nate's flesh. Fear mirrored in his eyes. His breathing slowed, then stopped, and his eyes glazed over, unseeing.

"Stop who?" Nate shouted. Heart racing, he punched in 911. "Don't die!"

Even as he said the words he knew it was too late. Coach Riley was gone. But he'd seen people being revived in the movies. The paramedics made it look easy. And there was that time when he was eight and had fallen down the stairs. His parents said he'd died and had to be revived, but he'd always thought they were overreacting and trying to scare him into being more careful.

The call picked up. "This is 911. What is your emergency?"

"Need an ambulance at Pinedale High School." His voice trembled. "Hurry."

He heard the basketball players running down the hall in the direction of Riley's office.

"Who screamed?"

"Was someone hurt?"

Students crowded into the office entrance, all talking at the same time.

Then one of them screamed, and another one fainted.

Nate felt numb. He laid Riley gently on the floor and stood. Pushing past the students, he handed someone his cell with the instructions to finish the conversation with the 911 operator.

He needed air.

He knew he'd never be able to purge the image of Coach Riley from his mind. The poor man looked like someone had tried to burn him alive. Bile rose again in his throat. Who would do something like that? Then there was the coach's confession and pleading with him to stop someone before he killed again. But who?

Coach Riley said he had killed Aaron. How was that even possible? Coach Riley wouldn't hurt a fly. He claimed it was not his fault. Someone had made him do it. No, that wasn't right. The coach had said, "*It*." Nate shivered. Mrs. Waters had talked about a serial killer and rumors that it could possess its victims.

Nate retraced his steps through the basketball court. Word had spread about Riley, and students, teachers, and coaches swarmed into the gym. They wouldn't like what they found. He should tell them. He couldn't. He felt sick.

He pushed through the double doors of the gym and jogged toward the track as students rushed past him. The bitter taste in his mouth returned with a vengeance.

He bent over and threw up his breakfast.

Chapter Twenty-Four

Police vehicles, firetrucks and aid cars crammed the school's parking lot near the football field. Nate perched on the bleachers, watching the show as though it was a scene from a movie. It didn't seem real.

Men and women in uniform or dressed in suits crowded over the school grounds, interviewing students, suggesting counselors to those who had seen Coach Riley's charred body or heard the description. They'd asked Nate the same questions, offering the same advice about seeking a counselor and since he had been the one to find the body, they'd told him not to leave.

He pressed both heels of his hands against his pounding headache. Exactly where did they think he'd go? He heard the caw of ravens and looked up. Edgar and Allan had settled on the bleachers above him a short distance away.

"Sorry, fellas, I don't have food for you today."

Edgar hopped over to Nate and deposited a shiny gold pendant beside Nate. The pendant was caked in dirt, partially covering up what looked like numbers engraved in the metal.

"Cool. You got me a gift. I needed that today. Thanks, guys."

"Mr. Collier."

Detective Morrison climbed the bleachers, approaching Nate as though he were a scared animal he needed to approach with caution. "Been looking for you."

Nate pocketed the pendant and just nodded. He didn't have the energy for a snappy response.

"This murder is a strange one," Detective Morrison said as he sat down beside Nate. "Can't figure out how the assistant coach managed to burn himself without torching everything else around him. But that's not my department. We'll do an autopsy. Preliminary report points to suicide, on account of the note."

"A suicide note?" Nate said evenly. "That was considerate."

Morrison looked over at Nate, finished writing, and tucked his pen behind his ear. "In the note he also admitted that he killed Aaron and was the sole person behind the test cheating ring. Mystery solved and still time for me to get home for dinner with the family. All in a day's work."

"Congratulations. You have Aaron's killer and the person behind the ring all wrapped up in a neat bow. Anything in the note about him torching the library or causing the earthquake?"

Detective Morrison tucked his notebook into the inside pocket of his suit. "No, but we're still looking into a connection."

Nate nodded. "Well, if you'll excuse me, I'm meeting my friends in town."

"One thing that bothers me. I never liked presents tied up with neat bows, or cases that were considerate. They give the impression that someone is trying too hard to impress, or in this case distract. I like the bows my kids tie on my presents. There's no pretense. No ulterior motive."

"You don't believe the assistant coach was the killer?"

"Do you?"

"You asking my opinion?"

"I am."

Nate leaned back against the bleachers. "Okay, here goes. I'll tell you what I told the police. Coach Riley wasn't completely innocent. But you were right when you said this was a strange one. He was scared and told me that someone forced him to kill Aaron. I don't believe Riley was working alone. And then there is the way his body was burned. Nothing else in his office showed burn marks. With a fire hot enough to burn his body like that, you would have thought the flames would have at least jumped to the desk."

The detective smiled. "I knew there was a reason I liked you. You're thinking like a real detective. You might reconsider going to college after you graduate."

"How did you know I hadn't planned on attending college?"

"I'm a detective, remember? It's my business to know random things about anyone involved in a crime. For instance. I've seen my share of burn victims in the past. Riley's burns aren't consistent with what I've seen. It's as though he was burned from the inside out. My advice, young man, is for you and your friends to be careful. My guess is that the killer is still out there and desperate. Trying to pin this murder on the assistant coach *and* link him to the test score ring was sloppy."

"How so?"

"Like I said before, when a case is tied up in a neat bow, it makes detectives like me suspicious." Detective

Morrison handed Nate his card. "Be careful, and if you need anything, just contact me and I'll come running."

Chapter Twenty-Five

Air currents settled around the football field, casting the funnel of light near the excavation site in shades of gunmetal gray. The funnel shivered, blowing in the wind, then strengthened and formed into a translucent image of a young woman whose hair flowed down her back in dark waves.

Fiona kept her form transparent as she glided to the rooftop of the castle and hovered. Although an overcast day, the daylight would help camouflage her form. If someone glanced her way, they would see through her to the forest and believe they only imagined the outline of a young woman.

The living believed ghosts materialized only at night, but they were most plentiful during the daytime, as sunlight gave them more protection from inquisitive eyes. Fiona had come outside to think and escape her father's pacing. She was also curious about the fire. How soon would the living realize the identity of the person responsible for the fire was connected to the deaths?

And if they did find out, would her home be buried again, trapping her and her father inside?

Since the work at the excavation site had ceased, the place was quieter and more peaceful than it had been when the construction crews were here with their loud equipment and constant noise. One positive aspect of their digging was that it had freed her and her father from their prison when the construction workers unearthed the castle and removed the iron roof.

The wind changed and a conspiracy of ravens lifted from the trees, indicating that someone approached. Most of them headed toward town, but two broke off from the rest, circling over the young man called Nate as he walked in her direction. They must be the ravens Nate had named Edgar and Allan.

She had observed that he took great pains to have students and teachers believe that he wasn't interested in learning. He skipped school, disdained joining clubs, and passed just enough classes to remain eligible to run track. Yet he helped his mother in their movie theater in town, was an avid reader of mystery and thriller novels, even naming the ravens he had befriended after his favorite author, Edgar Allan Poe.

There was more to Nate than met the eye.

She had been inside the school when she saw Nate discover a manila envelope in a locker. She did not know what it meant, but Nate believed it was important and had kept it a secret.

With the birds following him, Nate jogged past the excavation site in the direction of the woods behind the bulldozed visitors' bleachers. He was persistent. She knew only one other person who had risked this much to right a wrong. Would Nate meet the same end? It had been foolish to make her presence known to him, and yet...

"Daughter, you should not have allowed that young man to see you," a stern voice admonished. "It started a chain of events that might end badly for us all."

Fiona jumped at the accusation in her father's voice. It was the same comment he had made for days. "Why must you always sneak up on me?" Even in death she could not escape his controlling ways.

"I did no such thing. I am concerned. I fear your good sense has been dulled with the passage of time."

She turned toward her father. Like herself, he wore clothes common in Scotland three or four hundred years ago. His kilt, proudly worn, was a red-and-black tartan in the plaid worn by the MacGregor clan. He, and the castle, were her only link with the world she had known before her death, but she and her father rarely spoke. He was a man buried in his secrets.

"Why do you stare at me?" Her father demanded, unable to hold her gaze.

"You chased Nate out of our castle. I feared you meant him harm. Why?"

"The young man is a threat to us."

"Father. We are dead. No one can harm us."

"You do not understand."

"Then explain it to me. Please. What are you so afraid of?"

Her father's form shimmered in the dying afternoon light, dissolving into threads of gray mist. He would spend the day, and the night as well, brooding. Fiona sighed, realizing that interacting with Nate had dredged up her own negative thoughts.

She had buried the events surrounding her death as though pushing them down would cause her less pain. Her father might have been responsible for Jeremy's death, but it was she who had known their love was doomed from the start. She was to blame for Jeremy's death. She should have discouraged his attentions, but she had been so caught up in their forbidden love, and their dreams of running off together, that she had ignored the dangers closing in on them.

She lifted her gaze to follow Nate's progress. He had reached the perimeter of the woods and disappeared into its shadows. Fiona had not realized how much she wanted to see Nate again. His courage reminded her of Jeremy's as she followed Nate into the heart of the forest, making sure she kept a safe distance from him. She did not want him to sense her presence.

A pang of guilt pressed against her chest as she conjured Jeremy in her thoughts. The living believed that ghosts never experienced pain. A foolish myth. Ghosts might have escaped physical pain, but trapped in this realm, their heartache, guilt, and regret only grew more severe. Hers threatened to tear her apart.

A movement in the woods caught her attention. The shadow of a large man advanced through the trees, and from this distance she was uncertain if the entity was a living or a newly formed ghost. It was not her father; of that she was certain.

Her father moved like liquid silver, whereas this being looked agitated and its movements uncertain. In the center of a clearing, it paused, then crouched down on its hands and knees as though searching for something. Could a new ghost have made an appearance without her knowledge?

The possibility was likely. The construction workers had exposed more than her home. They had unearthed a cemetery, with markers and tombstones that dated back centuries, as well as beginning the demolition of an old mausoleum on Cemetery Hill.

She and her father had died in a castle in Scotland and had been confined there until a wealthy landowner purchased the ruin and had it transported by ship to the colonies. She often wondered if the man would have bought their castle in Scotland and had it rebuilt in the New World if he had known it was haunted.

But it was the cemetery on the hill she was most interested in now, not the past. She had been observing strange glows of light coming from its direction for months. Had the dead been awakened? Or worse, was it evidence of the malevolent, deformed ghost that haunted the dead as relentlessly as it did the living?

A twig snapped, followed by loud cursing, and she recognized Nate's voice, coming from the direction of the path that circled Raven Lake. Who—or what—the entity was, it had heard Nate as well and delayed its search as it glanced in Nate's direction. As it did so, she caught a glimpse of its eyes. They glowed like embers in a banked fire, confirming her worst fears. The Nuckelavee had returned. She had thought it had been destroyed, or at least imprisoned as she and her father had been.

It rose slowly as Nate emerged from the path.

But its presence had not gone unobserved. The two ravens she had seen earlier flew toward it, diving at its head and pecking the exposed skin on its arms and neck. The entity roared, covering its face against the raven's attack. The ravens only intensified their assault. Bloodied and bruised, the entity broke into the shadows of the trees and disappeared.

Nate jogged into the clearing. "Fiona? Are you here?"

"Yes, my lord."

"What was all the commotion about? The ravens took off after that guy as though he were some sort of boogie man." Nate turned around in a full circle in his effort to locate where her voice had originated.

A heart-stopping smile spread across his face and Fiona thought she had never seen anything as wonderful. His smile was warm and welcoming. No judgment reflected in his eyes, no signs of disappointment, which were so common in her father's expression. Nor were there signs of the fear she'd seen with so many of the living when they encountered ghosts. He was extraordinary.

Fiona shimmered into sharper focus. Their connection was strong. She wanted that to be a good thing. He had called the entity a boogie man. She heard the laughter in his voice. He had meant his comment as a joke. Did he realize how close to the truth he had come?

"I am over by the cypress trees, my lord."

"I thought I told you to call me Nate," he said, smiling as he strolled over to her.

"You did, and I will try to remember," she replied, welcoming the joy she felt at seeing him. It would not last, she cautioned, hearing her father's words in her thoughts. "Your friends Edgar and Allan chased off someone they consider a threat."

He laughed, shaking his head. "Yeah, they're great. I'll remember to pack hard-boiled eggs in my lunch tomorrow. And crickets, if I can find them. That's their favorite." Nate glanced in the direction the entity had run. "Any idea who he was?"

Should she tell him? What if she were wrong? Her father said that just evoking its name brought danger.

Nate had gone to the area where the entity had searched. "Whoever he was, he was combing this place as though he were looking for something." Nate knelt on his haunches, examining the packed ground.

She joined him in the area he was studying. "What are you looking for?"

"I'm not sure. What I found, however, were drops of fresh blood. They could belong to the guy Edgar and Allan chased away. They were attacking him with a vengeance. Or the blood could belong to an animal."

She moved in closer. "This was the place where your friend was attacked and murdered. It could be Aaron's blood."

Nate jerked his head toward her. "Aaron was hanged. It can't be Aaron's blood. The coroner said the only marks on him were rope burns around his neck. Besides, this is fresh blood."

"There was a fight first," she said evenly, bracing for his reaction. Would he ask her why she hadn't helped Aaron? What answer could she give that he would understand? Ghosts were not allowed to intervene in the lives of the living. And yet, wasn't that what she had been doing since she'd met Nate?

Nate brushed fallen leaves from the area where the entity had been searching. "If Aaron was ambushed, his attackers might have left a clue to their identity. That must have been the reason that guy was here. There were two men the night Aaron was killed. Coach Riley confessed he was there. My guess is that the man the ravens ran off was either the second man or someone else." Nate removed small rocks from the area where the man had been searching. "I found something." He held up a gold chain with a broken clasp. "This might have belonged to the killer. Aaron never wore jewelry. Are you sure you don't remember what the men looked like?"

Lowering her head, she shook it slowly, wringing

her hands together. She could at least share what she knew and hope that would be enough to satisfy him. "I do not know who killed your friend. As for the entity…"

"Entity? Are you saying it was a ghost the ravens chased away? Unless ghosts have started bleeding, whatever it was is very much alive and injured."

She wrung her hands together again and began pacing in the clearing. Birds chirped in the trees and a fish leapt from the lake, splashing as it reentered. Normal and blissfully calm things that did nothing to soothe her. There must have been a reason why she could communicate with him so easily, when she had never been able to speak with a living before.

Perhaps helping him would help her move on. If she did move on, would she be reunited with her Jeremy again? The thought gave her courage. It couldn't hurt to tell him everything she knew. The knowledge might keep Nate safe. She'd failed Jeremy and withheld the seriousness of the threat against him, and it had cost him his life. She wouldn't make that mistake again.

She moved closer to Nate. "The men who killed Aaron wore masks. Neither of them resembled the entity you saw. If I am correct, it is something you cannot defeat. It is called the Nuckelavee. He is a vengeful ghost who can possess the living."

"Possession?" Nate laced his hands on the back of his head and circled Fiona. "Coach Riley wasn't acting like himself. No, just thinking he might have been possessed sounds bat-crap-crazy. But I've heard the name Nuckelavee before. Mrs. Waters told Ruth Ann, Carl, and me that there was a serial killer by the name of Mr. Nuckelavee. It can't be the same person. That would mean this thing you describe is impossibly old."

Light glinted in the waning light and slashed through the air, hitting Nate on the back of the head. He groaned and pitched forward as blood gushed from the wound.

She whirled around. "Father. What have you done?"

Her father stood a short distance away, holding a sword. "It is time to go, daughter." Her father drifted nearer. "You were becoming too attached to the young man. You risk his life telling him about the Nuckelavee, and you put us all in danger. This warning will serve as a deterrent for you both."

She bent down to examine Nate. "He still breaths, no thanks to you. Why did you attack him? Danger? We are ghosts. We are dead and confined to this world. What more can happen to us?"

"Foolish child. It was because of the Nuckelavee and his thirst for vengeance that the Pinedale citizens took the drastic measures they did, imprisoning him in a mausoleum and us beneath an iron roof. Do you want that to happen again?"

"It is you who are foolish. If it is the Nuckelavee, it may already be too late. But why must you harm those who get close to me?" Buried memories rose with the speed of light. She allowed them to flow freely, fueling her anger. "We have not spoken of the night Jeremy and I died, and I allowed myself to push down the past. But it is not forgotten, nor is it forgiven."

Her father winced, averting his gaze. "Jeremy was a man without property or family. He came from the Northern Isles of Scotland, without a penny to his name. He aspired to wed you to steal my wealth. It was my duty to protect you. We fought…"

"You failed to protect me," she said as tears blurred

her vision. "You stole my happiness."

He reached out his hand to her, but she pulled closer to the unconscious Nate, dimming her image until it was no more substantial than wisps of smoke from a dying fire.

"You killed the man I loved and my reason to live." She blinked away the tears that burned her eyes at the memory of finding Jeremy's body in the tower. She had known her father disapproved of their intended marriage and feared Fiona would run off with Jeremy, but in her naiveté, she had never expected her father would kill the man she loved to keep them apart. It was her fault Jeremy had died.

The despair and anguish she experienced had been so profound she had drunk a vial of poison and lain down beside Jeremy. She believed they would be reunited in death, but that was not her fate. When she awoke in her ghost form, Jeremy was gone.

"You and I are doomed to spend eternity tethered to each other and this castle, neither forgiving nor forgetting. I loved Jeremy and he loved me. He never cared about your money. We planned to run away to the colonies and start a new life."

"You are mistaken. There was pure evil in that young man's eyes when he thought no one was watching. But I should have foreseen how deep it ran. If I had only known…"

She heard Nate's ragged breathing as he pushed to a sitting position and gingerly touched the back of his head where her father had hit him with the hilt of his sword. She had hoped with time she and her father would find a way to resolve their troubles, but they only grew farther apart, he with his guilt and she with her anger.

Her father reached for her again. "We will talk later. In time you will understand my actions were only in your best interests and find it in your heart to forgive me."

She shook her head slowly. "We must learn to forgive ourselves first."

Fiona watched as her father retraced his steps to the excavation site. His form became translucent and disappeared in the autumn breeze. A sense of alarm struck her at his retreat. He had been able to wield his sword with such force that it had knocked Nate unconscious. What else had he been able to accomplish? Had he had any involvement in Aaron's death?

If the Nuckelavee had resurfaced, he could assume any form, possess any living body. She had never heard of him possessing a ghost. Was it possible that he had somehow learned how to inhabit her father's ghostly form?

Nate grimaced. "My head feels like it will explode, and I'm bleeding. Who hit me? Did that entity, as you called him, return?"

Fiona knew it was time to face the truth. She had been locked for hundreds of years in a state where she denied that she lived with a monster. "You should know the truth. Ghosts have a violent, unpredictable side." She hesitated, weighing her words. "My father struck you with his sword."

"How is that possible? I've heard of ghosts rattling a few chains, but whacking people with swords is a new one on me."

Fiona watched as Nate processed this new information. She could almost guess what he was thinking, and she dreaded his next question—a question she had started asking herself.

"Did your father kill Aaron?" Nate said, leveling his gaze.

The tears she had held in check filled her eyes. "I…I cannot be sure. You deserve answers, and we must leave this place and get closer to the water. There we will be safe."

Chapter Twenty-Six

Nate scooped up the broken chain he had dropped when he had been hit over the head and shoved it into his pocket. He must be mentally unhinged, Nate thought as he followed Fiona's white flowing form to the shoreline of Raven Lake. Fiona had promised him answers. He had a feeling he might not like what she had to say, especially when she had mentioned that they were safer in the water. What was that about?

The stars and moon were hidden behind thick threatening clouds. His head throbbed from the blow he'd received from her father. He had no idea where Carl was. He didn't know why a packet full of teachers' answer sheets and what looked like legal documents had been so important that they had been stashed in their secret locker. He felt certain the contents of the envelope connected somehow to Aaron's murder.

Then there was the cryptic comment Aaron had given him. *Do not trust anyone.*

"We are very close," Fiona whispered.

Nate jogged to keep up with her, each step reminding him of his splitting headache.

"We are here." Fiona announced as she stopped abruptly. "The Nuckelavee does not like the water."

Her sudden stop caused him to pass through her. He landed on the ground with a thud.

"Ouch!" he said, glaring at her wispy form. Dealing

with a ghost was unsettling. Although he could still make out her features, he saw rhododendron bushes and squirrels bustling up maple trees through her transparent form.

It creeped him out. He clamped down on his teeth to keep them from chattering. He should have gotten used to seeing her this way by now, but sometimes he was caught off guard. The feeling of anxiety in the pit of his stomach was worse than when he had gone on the roller coaster ride at the amusement park when he was five. He'd thrown up a hot dog and a particularly large amount of sickly-sweet-tasting purple cotton candy. To this day he couldn't think of either without an accompanying urge to retch.

"Are you unwell?"

"I'm fine," he said, suppressing a smile as he remembered his father's definition of the word "fine." His father said the letters in the word stood for Freaked out, Insecure, Neurotic, and Emotional. The word summed up how he was feeling right now.

"Only my pride. I should have watched where I was going. If you had been human, I would have run into you. As it was, I ran through you as though you were no more substantial than a cloud of smoke. I need to pay better attention." He scrambled to his feet and dusted leaves and twigs from his jeans. "What is a Nuckelavee? Mrs. Waters, at the Ghost Whisperer store, claimed he was a serial killer."

She glided over to the edge of the water. "The actions of a Nuckelavee would appear as those of a serial killer. He takes possession of a living being, be it human or animal, to gain power. But the more the human or animal fights the possession, the faster their body burns out and dies. There are many Nuckelavees in Scottish folklore. Some are like Scotland and Ireland's horse demons that lure people to their deaths, while others cause plagues and diseases. The one my father and I believe followed us from Scotland can possess any living creature and make it do unspeakable things."

"Like kill Aaron? You think it might have inhabited your father?" Nate said.

She turned to face him. "Possibly. And that is what scares me. If it is the Nuckelavee, you cannot win. The town was able to defeat him once through trickery. Perhaps you should let them try to do it again."

But even as he put together a logical reason to let others find Aaron's killer, he knew he couldn't just stand by and do nothing. This afternoon had been a prime example, after Coach Riley's gruesome death. He'd told the police that the coach had said a ghost was involved. They'd dismissed his story as the delusion of a dying man. No, this was something he had to do.

An uneasy feeling gripped him as he walked behind Fiona. His hand closed around the pendant in his pocket. He hadn't thought about it until now, but it had been a weird coincidence that Edgar and Allan had given it to him right after Coach Riley's death. The pendant's image flashed in his thoughts. He had seen it before, but where? It couldn't be a coincidence.

Intent on trying to remember where he'd seen the pendant, he brushed against Fiona's translucent ice-cold form. Shaken, he shuddered. The emotions he'd felt when he'd fallen through her cloud-like form flooded back, more unsettling than he cared to admit. In both instances he had been forced to admit she was out of reach. He was struck with the cruel irony that Fiona was the first girl for whom he had ever been able to sustain more than a few days' worth of interest, and she was a ghost.

The glint of steel arced toward him. He ducked, feeling a whoosh of air above his head.

"Father!" Fiona screamed, her voice filled with panic. "Stop this at once!"

"I cannot," MacGregor said. His voice was devoid of emotion as he gripped the hilt of the blade tighter. "If what we suspect is true, and the Nuckelavee has returned, this young man must learn how to defend himself."

"Say what?" Nate glanced between Fiona and her father.

"His name is Nate, and he does not need to fight the Nuckelavee," Fiona said.

"If the Nuckelavee is who I believe he is, Sir Nate will not have a choice."

"I am not a knight, sir."

"You will be able to fight like one when I'm through."

MacGregor held a two-fisted sword that looked as long as MacGregor was tall. Nate, Aaron, Ruth Ann, and Carl were familiar with swords. It was yet another thing they had in common. They spent weekends playing the game Dungeons and Dragons and attending medieval fairs.

But this was not a game. Fiona and her father were freaked out about this Nuckelavee, which freaked Nate out. But a sword?

Nate stepped forward. "Begging your pardon. Just a thought. Wouldn't a gun be more effective?"

Fiona's father looked toward his daughter. "Is he

mad? Bullets will not harm a Nuckelavee. Only iron has the power to hurt him."

Nate thought about pointing out that bullets could be made from iron, but he changed his mind. Fiona's father had the look of a man with a one-track mind.

"Are you ready?" MacGregor said, tossing the sword he held toward Nate.

The blade flashed through the air like molten silver. Nate's lightning-fast reflexes responded. He snatched the hilt before the blade touched the ground, then struck a warrior's pose.

"Well done." MacGregor retrieved a second two-handed sword he had leaned against a tree. "I have underestimated the young lord's skill. You must be familiar with this type of weapon to have been able to catch it so easily. I am impressed."

"My friends and I used to spend every waking hour on the greenbelt behind my house, playing war games and mock sword fights. I always played the part of the Black Knight."

"Well, let us see if your hours of practice have prepared you for me."

Without warning, MacGregor sliced his blade through the air. It was a tactic Nate knew was aimed at demoralizing a man's foe with a show of strength and skill. MacGregor was obviously extremely comfortable with a blade. But there was good news and bad news about fighting with a two-handed sword.

The good news was that the weight and length of the sword enabled a soldier to slice his opponent in two with one swing of the blade. The bad news was that the sword was so heavy fights never lasted long.

Nate had been truthful when he bragged about how

much time he and his friends spent in sword fights. The one piece of information they had neglected to tell their parents was that as they grew older, they had replaced their homemade wooden swords with ones made from steel.

The weight of the blade MacGregor had tossed Nate felt heavier than the one hidden in his attic. He liked the difference. It was a finer blade, and the weight suited him. But the absurdity of fighting MacGregor weighed more heavily on his mind than the sword he held. With his friends, they had blunted the blades, and had strict rules on ending a fight before someone got injured.

Nate harbored no illusions. MacGregor had the look of a man who fought to kill. Nate shrugged out of his jacket, tossing it over a fallen tree stump. "A question before we begin. Are you the Nuckelavee and did you kill my friend?"

"Those are two questions. No, upon my honor, no, I am not the Nuckelavee, and I did not kill your friend."

"And exactly why should I believe you?"

"You ask exceptionally good questions. There is no reason in the world you should believe me. I have given you no reason to trust me. I have been many things in my life, but I have never killed a man in cold blood. You do not have to believe me, but you do have to believe that your life and the lives of your friends and family are in jeopardy. Are you going to stand there all night talking?" MacGregor scoffed. "Or are you ready for battle?"

"How often can you die?" Nate taunted.

MacGregor laughed and answered by swinging his sword at Nate's head.

Nate blocked the blade with his own and the force vibrated through him as he drew back and maneuvered in position to press the attack. The clang of steel on steel echoed through the air.

"You fight well," MacGregor said. "Determined, single-minded. Good qualities in a knight. But you are green and inexperienced. I sense you lack the killer instinct." MacGregor lunged with renewed energy, grazing Nate's arm.

Warm blood trickled down his arm. Fool, he chided himself. He had been listening to MacGregor babble, allowing himself to be distracted. It was the same trick he had used successfully whenever he fought with his friends. It was time to display more than his skill with a sword. He had to fight smart.

Nate sidestepped, circling MacGregor. "You never answered my question. How often can you die?" The question took MacGregor by surprise, and he hesitated. Nate seized the opportunity and lunged.

MacGregor blocked Nate's attack, matching him blow for blow. "It is a question you will not have answered, for if you do not learn how to fight the Nuckelavee, it is you who will die."

"Will I die by the sword? Or do you intend to hang me like Aaron?"

MacGregor stepped back, lowering his weapon to his side. "Again. I. Did. Not. Kill. Your. Friend. I swear on my love for my daughter."

"And what of your daughter?" Nate said evenly, remembering the story Carl had told him regarding the legend of how Fiona had died.

MacGregor lunged toward Nate, grabbing him around the throat. "What is your meaning?"

Nate stood his ground. "You know exactly what I mean. According to legend, the castle was attacked, and many died by the sword. The legend claims that Fiona was either strangled or hung. You were discovered at the bottom of the cliffs below your castle. It was assumed that you murdered even those unarmed, felt remorse, and then committed suicide. There was a note, written in your own hand, confessing to all that you had done."

"I was promised that my daughter's life would be spared if I took the blame. Only later, in my ghost form, did I realize I was deceived and that she had taken her own life."

Silence descended over the forest, smothering the whispers of the wind through the trees.

"Father," Fiona said gently. "Why have you kept this from me?"

He sighed, sheathing his sword. "It wouldn't have made a difference. It is the time for a reckoning. Put your sword away. We will resume practice at this time tomorrow night. You must be ready. Through my actions, vengeance was released. I had only wanted to protect Fiona from a danger. Instead, I was the reason she died. When Jeremy asked for Fiona's hand in marriage, we fought, and he was gravely injured. I had only wanted to scare him away. I left to seek a physician, but I didn't get far. The rest, as you have said, young man, is resigned to legend, and there it should stay."

"Father," she whispered. "I did not know. I hated you, and for that I am sincerely sorry. You mentioned that someone forced you to take your own life. Do you know who it was?"

MacGregor's chin trembled as he nodded. "You are kind in your forgiveness, and I am grateful. Regarding my enemy, I have my suspicions and I pray I am wrong. No deaths are random. But please learn to find happiness." He turned toward Nate. "You must find your friend's killer, and soon." He turned and moved in the direction of the castle. He looked like he carried a century of regrets on his shoulders.

"Are you okay?" Nate asked, moving to Fiona.

She blinked the tears from her eyes. "For so long I have hated him. Now I must learn to love and trust again. But my father is correct. We must find the Nuckelavee."

"Easier said than done. I have more questions than answers, and the clues keep mounting. I don't know what is important and what is a false trail. I need time to sort it all out."

"Come with me," Fiona said. "I know a place where we will be safe."

Chapter Twenty-Seven

Fiona led Nate to a secluded alcove along Raven Lake, where the moon reflected on the mirror-smooth waters. A small rowboat was tied to a tree along the shore and waves lapped gently against its sides. Nate's winged companions, Edgar and Allan, had returned and perched on a limb that draped over the shoreline of Raven Lake, his self-appointed guardians.

He'd had a huge hole in his heart ever since his father left. He hated him for the emptiness he felt inside and blamed it for why he couldn't get close to people. But he had never experienced the horror Fiona must have felt. The man she had loved had been killed and she believed his murderer had been her father. That was a different level of pain.

He rolled up his sleeves and splashed ice-cold water from the lake over his wound to clean it and shivered, welcoming the cold. It helped to ground him that he was still alive, or still "a living" as Fiona would say. He swept his hair back over his forehead.

Fiona moved beside him and giggled.

Nate scrunched his eyebrows. "What's so funny?"

"You are wet. Most livings won't go near the water this time of year. The water is freezing."

"How about you? Do ghosts like water?" He was deliberately teasing her. He wanted to do something normal and pretend, if only for a brief time, that he and

Fiona were just kids having a good time.

"We do not like the water, especially the Nuckelavee, which is the reason I thought this would be a good place for us to talk." She cocked an eyebrow. "What are you doing? You would not dare…"

"I love a dare." He grinned, scooping water into his hands and tossing it toward her. As expected, it went straight through her form and drenched the underbrush behind her. This time it didn't bother him as much that her form wasn't solid. He supposed he was getting used to her being a ghost.

But even though the shock was less, seeing the water pass through her like that brought it all back into focus. If he tried to reach out and touch her it would be like trying to hold a fist full of smoke. He fought the dark cloud that seemed to hover over him whenever he had these thoughts. She wasn't real. What he felt for her… What was it that he felt? She was attractive, easy to talk to…and dead. That last part was the most important.

But this time he sensed she had felt the same thing as he had. Their relationship would never go beyond what it was now. They existed in two different realities.

She twirled a long curl, as though stalling for time. "You fought bravely. Did you know that no one has ever defeated my father in battle?"

"Technically, we called the fight off. But I'm glad I didn't know that bit of information before I agreed to play the Black Knight."

"Would it have made a difference?" Fiona asked.

"Not really."

Nate reviewed the gamut of emotions that had rattled around in his head when MacGregor tossed him the sword. His competitive nature had kicked in immediately. He had wanted to fight the man. Actually, he had wanted to defeat him, save the fair damsel, solve Aaron's murder, and live happily ever after…with a ghost.

He groaned. Counselor Williams would have a field day with that last admission. When he fought MacGregor, he'd felt invincible. It was good to have a cause and to be on the right side for a change.

The crisp night air chilled his bare skin and he reached for his jacket. As he bent to retrieve it, the pendant in his pocket slipped out. He had forgotten about it with everything else going on. He'd bet tickets to a weekend showing of a blockbuster movie that whoever was rummaging around on their hands and knees in the clearing had been looking for that pendant. If his logic held, it meant it was important.

He tried scrubbing away the hard-packed mud with his thumb. It was caked on like concrete. He plunged the pendant into the water, then cleaned it off with the sleeve of his sweatshirt and held it up to the moonlight.

On one side was Pinedale's python logo, and on the other side, the number thirty-three. The number thirty-three had been written on the manila envelope he'd found in the secret locker, as well. He sucked in his breath, recognizing the number.

Fiona glided over to him and looked over his shoulder. "Before we continue this conversation and you tell me what you found, I recommend we take the boat out on the water. I feel a great unease I cannot explain."

"The Nuckelavee is here?"

"Perhaps." She looked nervous and troubled. He could see the uncertainty reflected in her eyes.

"Okay. Let's go." His hands trembled as he put the

pendant back into his pocket. He untied the boat, waded into the water, and climbed in, using the oars to steer it out into the center of the lake. He didn't want to minimize her concern by commenting that he thought her unease, as she called it, had a lot to do with what she had experienced with her father. It was not easy to switch strong emotions off and on. It took time. Maybe it was that she sensed evil and wanted to get him to where it was safe. But his concern grew. He had never been comfortable on the water.

She had rematerialized opposite him on the boat the moment they reached the center of the lake. The water was calm enough that all he had to do was rest the oars and drift. She smiled and nodded, indicating that he should begin.

He cleared his throat, pulling the pendant from his pocket. "I wanted to ask you about this. It has the number thirty-three etched into metal." Saying the number out loud crystalized why he had thought it looked familiar. "Have you seen anything like this before? Say, on anyone who was around Aaron when he was attacked?"

When she shook her head, he continued. "When the football team won state last year," he said, trying to keep his voice steady, "the head coach gave each of the varsity players a pendant like this with the school's logo of a python on one side, and their assigned number on the reverse."

Fiona reached out to touch the pendant, then pulled back her hand as though realizing that she couldn't touch it even if she wanted to. "You believe it is connected to your friend's death. I cannot imagine why anyone would want to wear a number dangling from a chain. Diamonds, emeralds, or a strand of pearls, but not a silly number."

One side of her mouth edged upward at her attempt to lighten the mood. She must have sensed his distress. She'd asked why someone would wear a pendant like the one he talked about. A great question. Unfortunately, he'd seen the pendant a week before Aaron's death.

A wave rocked the boat gently, splashing water against the hull as a raven's caw sounded in the distance.

Nate bent forward and perched his elbows on his knees. He had learned, when he was trying to solve a problem or study for an examination, that changing topics or participating in an unrelated activity calmed his nerves.

His go-to methods ranged from reading to watching old black-and-white movies to running. As a result, when he returned to studying, he was more focused. Maybe explaining the obsession people had with athletic numbers to Fiona would help him make sense of the pendant's importance. Had the ravens found it at the scene of Aaron's murder? Or someplace else?

His stomach clenched. The sliver of dread he'd felt earlier now circled, tightened, then squeezed around him, making it difficult to breathe. "To answer your question, the number thirty-three on the pendant represents someone's sports number."

"Do people also have numbers instead of names in this century?"

How could he explain how athletes loved advertising their numbers, when the implications of his discovery spun out of control in his head? He pinched the ridge of his nose. He didn't like where this was going.

"Let me try to explain. People who participate in sports are assigned a number. Those numbers help to identify them on the field of play to those watching the sporting event. Also, if you have a favorite athlete you admire, you might wear his number on a sweatshirt, a shirt, or…"

"Or jewelry, like this pendant," Fiona finished.

"Exactly."

"And you remember who wore this pendant?"

"Right again," he said, his gaze traveling to the shore and the lengthening shadows.

The pendant had hung from Cindy's neck when she and Hinkle were dating. He remembered because Hinkle had made a big deal of giving it to her between classes. Hinkle had got down on one knee in the hallway and offered it to her as an apology for being such a complete jerk. He had begged her to take him back, and from the fact that she had accepted the pendant, it looked to the school like she had forgiven him.

He'd told Aaron about the exchange, and they had fought. Aaron insisted he had a chance with Cindy and accused Nate of wanting Cindy for himself.

But did that mean that Cindy had killed Aaron and lost the pendant in the fight?

He had to think this through. How could Cindy have overpowered Aaron?

It was true that she was athletic and strong and had competed in gymnastic competitions before she made the cheer squad. Even so, he doubted Cindy could have killed Aaron. She would have needed help. Had she asked Hinkle? But the bigger questions were why and how were the teachers' test scores connected?

Nate glanced toward Fiona. She had been unusually quiet and wore a confused expression. He didn't blame her. But her confusion was related to the sports numbers issue they had been discussing. Fiona had no frame of reference with which to compare. And then he was struck by a way to explain what he meant. On a calendar with photos of castles sold at the medieval fairs were pictured groups of men wrestling, jousting, and playing an early form of American soccer.

"Have you ever watched men joust?" he asked suddenly, breaking the silence.

"Of course. My father used to encourage all manner of contests involving physical strength and ability."

"Great. Now just imagine if the people involved in the contests had numbers painted on their suits of armor. It would make it easier to identify them. If someone wore a certain number, for example, he might think it brought him luck if he won, and then he'd want to wear the same number in the next contest."

"Are you saying the piece of jewelry you found represents a number someone wore in an athletic contest?"

Nate fingered the pendant and nodded. "This pendant belonged to a football player at Pinedale High, who then gave it to his girlfriend. I believe she lost it when she fought with Aaron. This might have been what the Nuckelavee was after."

Saying it aloud made it worse.

He took a moment to turn toward the shore, and as he watched, the shadows widened across the lake. A breeze had picked up and now brushed across the lake, creating ripples over the water. He replaced the pendant and then held onto the sides of the boat as it rocked back and forth slowly.

Nate glanced toward the darkening sky. "A storm's coming. We should head back."

"Just a little longer."

Nate nodded, refocusing on the pendant and its implications. He did not want to face the conclusion that someone he knew might be involved in Aaron's death.

But he knew Cindy and Hinkle and they knew Aaron. They weren't exactly friends, but neither were they enemies. They were just kids, trying to survive high school. How could either one of them want to harm Aaron?

An owl hooted from a tree along the shore, then lifted from the branches and soared overhead as it began its nightly hunt. Water rolled beneath the boat and bushes quivered as small animals and birds hid from the silent predator.

"It is not just the pendant," he continued. "It gets worse. I found an envelope in Aaron's locker. The envelope contained copies of teachers' test scores. I vaguely remember Aaron telling me there's an underground network run by someone on the football team. The purpose is to sell the tests to students at Pinedale High. If you are a top athlete, there is pressure to retain your status. Participation and excellence aren't enough. You have to maintain a C average in school to remain on the team. If you aspire to attending college, the stakes are even higher."

"Nate..." She glanced down at her folded hands. "Something my father said started me thinking, and I wanted to talk to you about it."

The rocking increased as waves pushed against the sides of the boat. Nate braced himself. She had been quiet, letting him ramble on and on about test scores and the pendant. She was a good listener. But her abrupt change of topic took him off guard. "Is this about your father?"

"No." She looked up at him. "A little. He advised that it was not too late for me to find happiness."

Overhead, Edgar and Allan circled the boat. Their screams rose in volume over a sudden gust of wind. They circled around and around at a dizzying speed as though trying to warn him. He gripped the sides of the boat tightly. "We need to return to shore."

"Do you like me?"

Warning bells clamored inside his head. Nothing good ever came from that kind of opening sentence. He dug his fingers into the boat's railing as the ravens screeched louder. Their cries were like fingernails on a blackboard. "Of course I like you. We're friends." The moment he said the words he knew they weren't what she wanted to hear.

Her mouth formed a thin line. "We are more than friends."

He clamped his mouth shut. Her expression looked as predatory as the owl's. Not good. How had he allowed himself to be lured out into the middle of a lake? "We should head back to shore," he said again as calmly as his racing heart would allow.

He reached for the oars, but before he could secure them, she knocked them out of his reach and into the water.

"I want us to be together forever."

Chapter Twenty-Eight

Fiona raised her arms and white-crested waves crashed over the sides of the boat. Water poured into the boat and rose up to his ankles.

Nate held onto the sides for dear life, sensing her intention to capsize the boat and drown him. Why hadn't he seen the signs? But how could he have guessed her reaction? This was his first ghost encounter. "Can we talk about this?"

"Join me in death."

"Are you out of your mind!"

"Very well." Her voice was dead calm as she raised her arms again. Waves swamped the boat.

Nate took a deep breath of air as he was tossed from the boat and into the churning water. Ice-cold currents surrounded him in a deadly embrace. Fiona floated below the surface as she descended deeper into the abyss, her arms outstretched toward him as she beckoned him to join her in death. She'd lied about being afraid of the water. What other lies had she told him?

He had never been a great swimmer. His mother described him as *water safe*. Which meant that he could float on his back and do a reasonable dog paddle in a swimming pool.

He sank lower through the waves. He was glad he had forgotten his jacket on the shore. At least it and the manila envelope would be found—by the right people, he hoped.

He was thinking rationally. That had to be a good thing. Right. Or was he just numb and had accepted his fate?

Underwater grass wrapped around him, trapping his legs, preventing him from kicking. His lungs felt like they were on fire. In minutes, he knew, he'd lose consciousness. Fiona had won. He would see her soon.

Anger swelled within him. How could she do this to him? You did not hurt the person you professed to care about. You protected them.

His thoughts sped to his mother. To Ruth Ann. Carl. What would they think? Would his mother be okay? Would she and his friends think he had committed suicide? Or would they believe that he had been murdered?

Chapter Twenty-Nine

Under the watchful gaze of the full moon, Raven Lake glistened in shades of midnight blue and pewter gray. Beneath the waves, Nate gazed toward the moon's glow through the underwater currents and their ever-changing colors, no longer feeling the strength to fight as he sank lower.

Arms circled around him, gathering him close.

His first thought was that it was Fiona, dragging him further to his death. But he was not going down. He was going toward the light. The sensation mirrored the times he'd almost died, only this time he would not wake up.

He watched his body break the surface as he was pulled through the water and laid on solid ground.

The shrill racket of hundreds of angry ravens pierced the frigid air. The sound seemed to come from a long way away, picking up speed with every second that passed. The earsplitting noise continued as a woman shouted for him to wake. The voice sounded like Ruth Ann's. Impossible. He was dead. A ghost. Fiona had won.

His head was tilted back, and his chin lifted. Someone pressed down on his chest in rapid succession. Then soft lips pressed against his mouth. He felt the gentle pressure. How was that possible? He was no longer alive. He wanted to lean into that kiss, but it ended abruptly and the chest compression began again.

His eyes snapped open and he coughed up water and rolled to his side, heaving up more water. Someone draped a coat over his shoulders and rubbed his back gently in circles.

"Please stay as still as you can. You will be okay. I promise."

He knew that voice. It sounded like the voice of an angel. "Ruth Ann." Relief, gratitude, love, all merged and swelled within him. He was alive. He rolled to a sitting position but swayed, feeling dizzy.

She draped her arm around his shoulders to keep him steady. "You are going to feel tired, short of breath, with a tightness in your chest. It will pass in a few days."

"I almost died and you're reciting lines from a lifeguard's handbook." He rubbed his chest trying to ease the sudden pain. It felt as though he'd been hit in the chest with a sledgehammer. "You know something about everything. How did I get so lucky to have a friend like you?" He folded her in his arms, fighting back tears. "You saved me."

She smiled against the side of his neck as she pushed to create a space between them. "Of course I saved you. That's what friends are for. Especially when I have friends who refuse to learn how to swim."

"I can swim."

"Splashing in the water does not count. What were you doing on a boat at this time of night, anyway? You almost drowned."

"Long story, full of embarrassing details," he said. "More to the point, how did you know I was here?"

She tilted her head toward Edgar and Allan, who were perched on a branch over his head. "Your friends found me and wouldn't stop screeching and yelling at me until I followed them. You owe them, big time."

"I owe you big time." Nate stood, feeling wobbly, and reached for her hand, pulling her to her feet before he grabbed his jacket and made sure the brown envelope was still inside. "We should get home and out of these wet clothes. I have a lot to tell you. But it's all disjointed."

She picked up her flashlight and looped her arm through his as they made their way down the path and through the woods toward the school grounds. "I was serious when I told you to take it easy for a few days."

"We don't have a few days."

As they walked down the path toward the school, she leaned her head against his shoulder, a habit he was beginning to love. "Unfortunately, you may be right. Carl showed up on my doorstep asking if I'd seen you. He was acting strange and wanted to come in. I told him my parents weren't home and that he should leave."

Nate glanced toward her, putting his hand over the one she rested on his arm. There was something in her voice that concerned him. Her tone had dipped lower and there was an edge of fear he hadn't heard before. "You let me into your house when your parents weren't home before."

"That's different. When my parents are gone, you always come over to check to make sure all the doors and windows are locked and bring me leftovers from your dinner." Ruth Ann aimed the flashlight at the forest path, illuminating the trail. "I can't put my finger on it, but there was something different about Carl. He was acting jittery, if that makes sense."

Nate remembered that Hinkle had described Coach Riley in a similar manner. "I'm glad you listened to your instincts regarding Carl."

"They've never steered me wrong."

He focused on the trail ahead, feeling a surge of protectiveness. Ruth Ann never overreacted. Ruth Ann was perfectly capable of taking care of herself. She had for years, but it had disturbed him that it didn't bother her parents to leave her alone when they traveled. "What did you tell Carl?" he asked evenly.

"At the time, I hadn't heard from you and was starting to worry. I sent Carl on his way because he was creeping me out. Then the ravens appeared, and one thing led to another, and here I am. Tell me about your news."

She had glossed over the exchange she'd had with Carl. He'd have a talk with Carl. That was not okay that he had made Ruth Ann uncomfortable. What was going on with the guy?

"I found the teachers' answer sheets in Aaron's locker, the ravens gave me a pendant I suspect belongs to Hinkle, and Fiona tried to drown me so that we could be together."

Ruth Ann stopped abruptly. "That bitch! If she weren't dead already, I'd kill her myself."

Nate chuckled and pulled her against his side, kissing her on the top of her head, though what he really wanted to do was kiss her on the lips. He'd had those lips on his when she had given him CPR. God help him. He wanted more. "I've never known anyone quite like you," he said, trying to clear his head of Ruth Ann and her lips. "I tell you a whole bunch of stuff and you focus on Fiona trying to kill me. By the way, I love you, Ruth Ann."

"I know." A blush warmed her eyes as she gazed toward him before quickly turning back to concentrate on the path. "The teachers' test answer sheets are at the core of Aaron's murder. We must flush out whoever is behind them. Do you have any ideas?"

"I'm working on it."

"Nate!" she suddenly shouted. "Look out behind you!"

****

He spun around in time to see Hinkle racing toward them on a dead run and then hurl himself in the air.

With Ruth Ann beside him, Nate twisted out of Hinkle's reach.

Hinkle landed a short distance away. The impact of his fall knocked the wind out of his lungs, and he moaned, struggling to stand.

"I'll take care of Hinkle. Contact Detective Morrison at the precinct. Talk only to Morrison. Tell him I have a lead on Aaron's killer. Go."

"I don't want to leave you alone."

"You won't be. The ravens are hanging out in the trees. If they think I can't handle Hinkle, they'll peck out his eyes. Now go."

"If you had told me a few days ago that Edgar and Allan had your back, I would have laughed in your face." She reached up and pecked him on the cheek. "Be careful."

Ruth Ann took off toward the parking lot as Hinkle, having regained normal breathing, straightened and moved toward Nate slowly. "I know you have them. They weren't in Aaron's locker, and Carl said he didn't have them anymore. I want those score sheets and the documents."

"Why don't you start with telling me who besides Coach Riley killed Aaron," Nate said, biding his time.

He wanted Ruth Ann far away. He'd told her he could take care of Hinkle, but that was only if Hinkle was Hinkle. If he was possessed by the Nuckelavee, that was another story.

The ravens circled overhead, distracting Hinkle as he waved his arms to drive them away. "What is with these birds?"

Nate observed Hinkle as he tried to avoid the ravens. He looked as he always had. Fiona said when the Nuckelavee possessed someone or something he burned the victim from the inside out. She hadn't said anything about a personality change, but that seemed likely as well. Hinkle didn't show any signs of being like Coach Riley, but he wasn't sure what he was looking for.

Fiona had mentioned the Nuckelavee had been around for centuries and was capable of possessing and turning people and creatures evil. The townspeople of Pinedale had called him a serial killer, and in a real way he was. They'd found a way to contain him, but then when construction work began around the school and Pinedale Cemetery Hill, the Nuckelavee must had been accidentally awakened.

The dead ravens Nate had seen right before he discovered Aaron's body had been the first clue. The Nuckelavee had possessed them and then moved on to humans. No wonder Edgar and Allan wouldn't leave his side. They knew about the Nuckelavee and wanted him destroyed as much as he did.

Who else had this thing possessed?

"I'm not sure who killed Aaron," Hinkle said, circling Nate. "All I was supposed to do was rough Aaron up enough that he'd turn over the test score sheets." Hinkle waved his arms again. "Get these ravens away from me!"

Ruth Ann had reached the parking lot and peeled away in her car toward town. She was safe. Nate signaled to the ravens to pull away. They complied but continued to circle overhead. He wasn't sure Hinkle was telling the truth or protecting someone because he was afraid. Either way, Hinkle belonged behind bars if he had anything to do with Aaron's murder. Absently Nate wondered how long it would take for the police to arrive. He could stall for only so long.

"You're right," Nate said. "I have the test score sheets, but you'll have to catch me first if you want them back."

Leaving Hinkle gap-jawed, Nate turned and headed back toward the boundary between the school grounds and the forest. His plan was to take the forest trail and then circle back. Hinkle outweighed him by at least thirty or forty pounds and might be a great quarterback and a passable sprinter, but Nate was one of the best distance runners in the state. His plan was to drag the race out as long as he could until the police arrived. The issue was that he wasn't at full strength after the near-drowning, but he was still faster than Hinkle.

The great unknown was if the Nuckelavee had possessed Hinkle's body. If he had, then Hinkle could easily run Nate down. Nate was hoping it was just Hinkle he ran against.

Nightfall had turned the vibrant autumn leaves of green, gold, and orange into the black and violet shades of a child's nightmare. Low-hanging branches reached out to slash his face. Twigs snapped underfoot, and a mist rolled in from the lake. He could barely see two feet in front of him as the forest closed in. He knew this trail like the back of his hand. He should—he had run it often enough. The football players rarely ventured this far from the football field and workout facilities. The majority of them weren't long-distance runners. He had that in his favor.

Nate lengthened his stride, and the distance between him and Hinkle grew. He knew Hinkle was still behind him. He could hear his labored breathing, interrupted only by loud cursing. Nate, on the other hand, hadn't felt this good in a long while. They called it a runner's high. Better than drugs, or so he had been told.

"Stop," Hinkle shouted through gasps of breath.

The arrogance in Hinkle's voice had been replaced by the powerful need to just hang onto the punishing pace Nate had set. They were alike in that way. Competitive to their core. Neither would quit once a contest started.

Nate knew Hinkle was listening to the sounds Nate made as he ran ahead. If Nate changed course, so would Hinkle. The best plan was to quicken his pace even more. It would force Hinkle to do the same, but he wouldn't be able to keep up. It would buy Nate time to spring into further action.

He quickened his pace and heard Hinkle groan with what must have been realization of the need to push to run even faster to keep pace. At the bend in the path that would lead back to the football field, Nate leaped for one of the branches on a maple tree and pulled himself up. He swung his legs around the stout limb to a sitting position and waited.

Hinkle slowed, pausing directly beneath the maple. Breathing labored, hands on his hips, he struggled to catch his breath. "You can't escape, and it's better if you deal with me and not the people I work for. Hand over the test score sheets and the documents. I'll tell them I found them. You'd be in the clear."

Hinkle sounded afraid, and after what had happened to Coach Riley he should be. Hinkle mentioned people he worked for, which suggested a well-organized gang. How deep did this cheating ring go? But Hinkle had also mentioned the documents. How were they involved? One thing Nate did know for sure was that whoever was behind the cheating ring was desperate enough to kill to keep it a secret. Time to turn over the rock and expose it to the world.

Nate leaped from the branch and tackled Hinkle, pinning him to the ground, taking him by surprise.

"What the…" Hinkle gasped for breath and fought to free himself, but Nate had him well pinned. "You have something that belongs to me," Hinkle said. He paused to take in a gasp of breath. "I need everything back."

"Not a chance, you piece of shit," Nate ground out through gritted teeth. "Why did you kill Aaron?"

Hinkle stopped fighting. His body went limp as he began to sob. He looked as though all the fight had drained from his body. His rage-filled expression crumbled. "I didn't kill Aaron. They weren't supposed to hurt him. I told them I'd convinced Aaron to return the test scores and documents to me and he promised to keep his mouth shut. He was supposed to meet me when it got dark, but he never showed up. You must believe me."

Nate eased away from Hinkle and stood. Nate had never seen Hinkle like this before. It was obvious he had not been taken over by some evil entity. All the bravado was gone. Nate had never seen him like this. Hinkle was the town's golden boy. He walked around the school with a perpetual smile and a swagger. He was Pinedale's undisputed king. Nate liked this version. Hinkle was real and really seemed like he had cared about Aaron.

"All I wanted were the test scores," Hinkle continued, swiping at his nose as he rose to a sitting position. "It all started the spring of my sophomore year. My grades were lousy, and I thought my dad would pop an artery. He wanted me to go to the same college he had, but even as a legacy preference there was no way without at least decent grades. I was desperate. Then Coach Riley approached me. It seemed so simple, and an answer to my prayers. But there was a catch. If I wanted the test scores, I had to sell them to other students."

"You were involved in the test cheating ring? You knew you could get suspended or kicked out of school. Riley and whoever else is involved might get jail time."

"Yeah, I thought of all that, but I never thought I'd get caught, and Riley said the cheating ring had been going on for decades, so not to worry. It didn't seem that big a deal, and I never got paid. All the money went to Riley. There were other teachers involved too, but I never knew who they were. I just figured it was no big deal. It wasn't hurting anyone."

"Except Aaron found out somehow and threatened to expose everyone," Nate said.

Hinkle hung his head. "Riley lost it. He said he'd lose his job and possibly go to jail, and he'd started counting on the extra money he earned from selling the test scores. I never got the feeling he'd go so far as killing Aaron to keep him quiet. I thought I had it under control. Aaron was going to return the test scores, and Riley said if Aaron kept quiet, he'd drop it and stop selling. Then, after football practice, shortly before I planned to meet

Aaron, Riley started acting strange. I've never seen him like that. He said he didn't care about the test scores anymore. It was something else in the envelope that he wanted."

"The documents?"

Hinkle nodded. "The last thing Coach Riley said to me was that if I didn't return the test scores and documents to him by the night of the lunar eclipse all hell will break loose. His exact words."

Nate hesitated. He'd heard that expression before. It was the night he'd discovered Aaron's body. It confirmed to him that Riley had been possessed the night of Aaron's murder. "That's the same night as Aaron's memorial."

Hinkle met Nate's gaze for the first time. "Riley's the reason I've been looking for you. I think someone killed Riley and is trying to tie up loose ends. I thought if I found the test scores and documents and left them in Riley's office, somehow whoever was in charge would find them. The hope was they'd leave both you and me alone. Two birds, one stone scenario."

Sirens wailed in the distance. The high-pitched sound grew closer and closer.

"Ruth Ann called the police. Well played. You were just stalling for time."

Nate hauled Hinkle to his feet. He believed Hinkle's story, and this time he did feel sorry for him. Hinkle had got caught up in something he didn't understand fully. An easy mistake, and if it hadn't been for Aaron's death, no one would have been the wiser. "You have to turn yourself in."

"Yeah, I know. I'm glad it's over." Hinkle looked at Nate. "You don't seem as angry. Does that mean you believe me?"

"You're making me a believer. Aaron's death wasn't your fault, and although it looks like Coach Riley killed him, it wasn't his fault either. He was possessed by the Nuckelavee. The only question would be that if the Nuckelavee is no longer possessing Coach Riley because the guy's dead, and he bypassed you for some reason, where did he go?"

"Come again? Nuckelavee who?"

In the distance, a half dozen police officers jogged down the path toward Nate.

"The police have arrived to take you into custody. I'll explain it all later. You'll have to go with them. Tell them everything you know. Don't leave anything out. I'm not sure what they'll do about the test scores and documents, but I'll square it with them regarding Aaron's death." Nate pulled the pendant and chain from his pocket and handed it to Hinkle. "Question. I found this in the clearing near Raven Lake. Tell me the truth. Don't lie. Was Cindy involved in this mess as well?"

Hinkle took the pendant and chain from Nate. "No, in fact Cindy threw the pendant back in my face the morning of Aaron's murder. I lost the pendant when Aaron and I fought. She learned about the test scores and…let's just say she didn't approve. Hey, why are you being so nice suddenly?"

"You're not such a jerk when you are being yourself. Remember what I said. Tell the police everything. I'll visit you later, but first I must find a way to rid the town of evil."

Hinkle grinned at Nate as the police approached. "If anyone else had made that comment, I would have had some snide remark. But all I can think about is that I wish

I could go with you."

Nate watched the police take Hinkle into custody. Hinkle had been forthcoming about everything and was glad it was over. Hinkle was wrong. It wasn't over. Not by a long shot.

Chapter Thirty

Nate stuffed his hands into his pockets and stood on the top steps of the bleachers. It felt like his go-to place when he needed time to think. He surveyed the parking lot and the football field as police led Hinkle to one of the squad cars. The pole lights in the parking lot had been turned on as well as the stadium lights, in preparation for Aaron's memorial celebration later tonight. As far as Nate was concerned, the lights' harsh, artificial glare exposed the danger the town was in. Something Hinkle had said kept revolving back into his thoughts. He'd said Riley didn't care about the test scores. It was the documents in the envelope he wanted.

The only other papers in the envelope were about how land was distributed both before and after the American Revolution. The last page outlined a land ownership dispute regarding the area where Pinedale High School, Pinedale Cemetery Hill, and Raven Lake were located.

Nate had been looking at Aaron's death through too narrow a lens, thinking he had been killed over test scores. The reason was bigger. Right now, the lands in dispute were owned by the city and designated for the use of the school and cemetery. What if someone could prove that they, not the city, owned the land?

Nate had learned in his science class that there were large deposits of pyrophyllite mineral still untapped in

North and South Carolina. Pyrophyllite was used in the pharmaceutical industry and in the making of plastics and paint. What if someone had discovered such mineral deposits on the school's grounds? Whoever owned the land would be a millionaire.

Land worth in the hundreds of millions of dollars was a reason to kill. A plan formed as to how he might be able to flush out both the killer and the Nuckelavee. He slipped the envelope from his jacket and separated the legal documents from the test scores, then put the test scores back into the envelope and folded and pocketed the documents.

It was several hours before midnight, and it felt as cold as the inside of the movie theater's walk-in freezer. Soon students would start gathering for Aaron's memorial service and the lunar eclipse tonight. He wondered if he would have any luck trying to cancel Aaron's memorial at this late date. Probably a waste of time. Everyone loved a party and any excuse he'd give, including paraphrasing Hinkle's words, that all hell was about to break loose, would only make the students more curious. Besides, he needed to flush out the Nuckelavee.

Hinkle was led in handcuffs to one of the squad cars as a black sports car pulled into the parking lot, followed by Ruth Ann's hybrid. He had meant it when he'd told Hinkle he'd check up on him later and put in a good word. And Nate had thought about texting Ruth Ann and telling her not to come because it was too dangerous, but he knew she'd just ignore his message.

But he was glad to see her. More than glad on many levels. He had a plan, and he needed her input to help put it into action. The black sports car had parked next to Ruth Ann. When Carl exited it, instead of the pile of junk he usually drove, Nate got a bad feeling. Carl and his mom weren't poor, but neither could they afford something as expensive as the sports car Carl had just driven up in. Where did Carl get the money?

But if Carl had received cash because he was involved in the cheating ring, why tell someone about it and risk exposing that he was involved by giving Nate the note about the secret locker?

He met his friends on the field, pulling Ruth Ann into his arms first, then Carl, because it would have been weird if he hadn't. Under normal circumstances he would have grilled Carl on where he had been. These weren't normal circumstances.

"It is great to see you, Carl. I got the note you slipped into your mother's brownies. That was smart."

"You found the test scores, then?" Carl's monotone, so unlike the animated voice he usually had, set Nate's teeth on edge. Not robotic, but close.

"Sure did." Nate removed the manila envelope from his jacket and held it in his hand, watching Carl's eyes grow brighter. "I forgot to give them to Officer Tinkler when he came to arrest Hinkle. They're the test scores and evidence. Do you think you could run them in to him at the precinct? Ruth Ann and I must help prepare for Aaron's memorial this evening."

He caught Ruth Ann's questioning stare, but she kept silent. A benefit of knowing someone all your life was that they could read your emotions like a book. She had sensed that Nate was lying.

Carl licked his lips. "Be happy to deliver this to the police station." He reached for the envelope and then hesitated. "It's sealed."

Nate nodded. "I thought it best to reseal the

envelope. That way the police won't think we tampered with it or tried to change anything inside. Think of it like that time in fourth grade when I asked you to pass that cute girl with pigtails a Valentine's Day card. We thought it would be best if the card was sealed. That made it look more official. Do you remember her name? Tall, athletic, played catcher on the softball team?"

Carl focused on the envelope. "Not sure I remember," he said absently as he spared a glance toward Nate.

Nate lifted the corner of his mouth. "Her name was Nancy Gallagher. She sat in front of me, and I used to pull her braids."

"Nancy?" Carl said as his voice dropped an octave lower. "Nancy. That's right. Now I remember. I'll do it. I'll make sure I give this to Officer Tinkler. When do you want to meet up again?"

Nate rested his hand on Carl's shoulder. It was unnaturally warm. "Let's meet at the cemetery around eleven thirty. We can say a few prayers over Aaron's grave before we meet back here for his memorial. Don't be late."

"I won't."

Nate blew on his hands to cool them as he watched Carl make the return trek to the parking lot. Carl felt like he was burning up. The empty feeling in the pit of Nate's stomach grew, opening the raw, bleeding grief he had felt when Aaron died. There was something seriously wrong with Carl. He had lost one friend. Had he lost two?

Carl got into his car and peeled out of the parking lot in a cloud of gravel. Carl never drove recklessly. He was Mr. Cautious. He'd never had a speeding ticket. The only time Carl had been pulled over was to caution him that he had been driving too slowly.

Nate shuddered. More confirmation. Ghosts surrounded him, and not all of them were friendly.

"That was odd," Ruth Ann said, coming up alongside him and following his gaze. "First, why did you lie to Carl? There is no such person named Officer Tinkler at the police station. Won't that get Detective Morrison's attention?"

"I hope so."

"And second, you told me that giving Valentine's Day cards was lame, and third, I don't remember a girl by the name of Nancy Gallagher in any of our classes."

"That's because I made her up. There wasn't anyone by that name in our school." He turned toward her. "You're wrong about one thing, though. I planned to give you a Valentine's Day card that year. Or I would have if I had gotten up enough nerve."

She ducked her head, but not before he noticed a soft, pink blush staining her cheeks. "What are we going to do?"

He knew she was talking about more than just Carl. She was talking about the two of them. He felt on edge, like he was standing on a cliff about to be blown over by a stiff wind if he made the wrong move. He needed a long run. That always cleared his head. "I don't know yet."

He and Ruth Ann were friends. Good friends. If they didn't work as a couple, would that ruin their friendship? The odds were that it would, and he was unwilling to take that leap. He cared for her too much and wanted her in his life.

"You suspect Carl of being the Nuckelavee," she

said breaking into his thoughts. "That explains the strange feeling I've been having about him."

"If I'm right about Carl, we're going to need help. I know your parents are still out of town, but do you think you could call them and see if they can do us a favor?"

"What do you have in mind?"

"I'd like you to ask them if they can work their lawyer magic on a couple of things. The first is to get Hinkle released tonight, and the second is to look over a document I plan to scan and email them."

Chapter Thirty-One

Nate was the first to arrive at Pinedale Cemetery Hill.

Meeting here where a week ago Aaron had been buried seemed appropriate somehow. At the moment, a full moon hung overhead, resting in a pillow of stars. It looked peaceful and serene. Looks were deceiving. The wind rustled the trees and the branches rattled like the bones of the dead, foreshadowing a storm. The ravens were restless, as though sensing danger, confirming Nate's worst fears.

Tonight was a crossroads. Whatever happened would shape the school and the town of Pinedale, for better or for worse, for years to come. Nate had never wanted to be thrust into this position. He wasn't the guy who leapt before the starter gun went off at track meets. He was the guy who waited for the signal for the race to begin.

He walked over toward Aaron's grave. When Aaron's casket had been lowered, Nate looked away. He couldn't watch. That would make it real. It still didn't seem real. It didn't help that he had been able to see Aaron as a ghost by the school lockers. Nate didn't know if that had been good or bad. Would it help the grieving process to be able to talk to Aaron? That was for a counselor to determine, he supposed. But it also meant that Aaron couldn't move on, and that wasn't right either.

He and Aaron had only spoken through Fiona, and that had been to ask Aaron if he knew who had killed him. That was Nate's fault. He was afraid to ask him how he was doing.

Nate knelt beside the grave. No, that wasn't it either. He wanted to say he was sorry for the fight they'd had.

Aaron floated into view. His expression was as somber as Nate felt. No one underestimated what was at stake. If this plan failed, Aaron would remain a ghost for eternity. He would never have the chance to reconcile what held him in the world of the living and be able to move on and unite with loved ones. He would be stuck.

And what about Carl? What would become of him? He had been possessed by the Nuckelavee, a being that had taken over Coach Riley and now possessed Carl. Nate had to find a way to get the Nuckelavee to release Carl before it was too late.

Friends don't abandon friends.

Ruth Ann had said those words the day of Aaron's funeral, and she was right.

The mantra whispered in the breeze. It rustled the fallen leaves into mini wind tornados, reminding him that if he hadn't been angry with Aaron and had met him on time at the track, things might have been different. He couldn't change the past, but he could do something about the present.

"We want to talk to you before the others arrive," Aaron said. "We have an idea, but there is a risk." Aaron's voice was distant as though he had addressed Nate as a stranger rather than a close friend. And when he had said, "We have an idea," Nate got the impression he didn't mean he and Nate.

Nate swallowed hard. He figured Aaron was dealing with some really tough stuff and had to keep that part of him that connected him to being alive at a distance. It hurt that Nate couldn't help his friend. Maybe if they survived tonight there was a chance to repair their friendship before Aaron moved on. Nate had to hope that was possible.

Nate focused on Aaron's semi-transparent form. "When you say, 'we,' exactly who do you mean?"

"I'm talking about Fiona."

"You know she tried to drown me so that, and I quote, *We could be together forever*. How creepy is that?"

Aaron glanced toward a funnel of light that hovered a short distance away. "Pretty creepy. She told me and she's sorry. She was confused."

"Okay. If you mean confused in the sense that she can't be trusted, you're right."

"That is fair. But she and I have a plan."

Nate wanted to push back and tell Aaron no. But the truth was that he needed all the help he could get even if it meant working with Fiona. One thing was certain: he trusted Aaron. "What is the plan?"

Fiona glided over beside Aaron. "You should tell him."

Aaron glanced past Nate in the direction of the graves that lined the rolling hillside. "Here goes. Fiona has been filling me in on ghostly dos and don'ts, which might help us to defeat the Nuckelavee. We can walk through walls, cause things to fall from walls—"

"Drown humans?" Nate shut his eyes. "Sorry. Still fresh in my mind. Mrs. Waters said the Nuckelavee must come here tonight if he plans on remaining human. If that is the case, we don't have that much time."

"One more do," Aaron said. "We can raise the dead."

The air dropped in temperature. "So we will have more ghosts to worry about? That doesn't seem like a positive. Please tell me you haven't done this already. And how will that help us?"

Fiona wrung her hands, glancing toward Aaron again. "We wanted to ask you first, but we do think it is a good idea. We will need help to fight the Nuckelavee. He is strong and resourceful. We promise we will only raise good ghosts."

Nate almost laughed at her last remark but paused. "You're serious. You think you can distinguish between good and bad ghosts? Based on what? What is written on their headstone?" He shook his head. "It's too much of a risk."

"I didn't like the idea either, at first," Aaron said. "But Fiona said the newly dead are in a trance-like condition when they are first raised. Think of them like little children and Fiona and me as their parents. We feel certain they will listen to us when we order them to attack the Nuckelavee."

"It's a big gamble."

"What is a gamble?" Ruth Ann said, walking toward Nate, followed by Cindy and Hinkle. "My parents came through and arranged for Pete's release."

"Aaron said that Fiona showed him how to raise the dead and that will help us defeat the Nuckelavee."

"Cool." Ruth Ann's eyebrows snapped together. "Did Aaron say Fiona? What is she doing here? She tried to kill you."

"I don't like it either, but we need her help. If you're

okay, Aaron and Fiona will raise the dead. While that's happening, what have we learned about getting rid of the Nuckelavee?"

Ruth Ann crossed her arms over her chest and frowned. "I'm not okay with Fiona, but I'll cope. Here's what we've learned. If we fail at expelling the Nuckelavee, the town of Pinedale will be his next target. No one will be safe. So, no pressure."

Ruth Ann withdrew the book Mrs. Waters had given them from her backpack. "I've read over the instructions on how to banish a ghost. There are a few suggestions, mostly associated with cleansing your house with sage and herbs so the ghost won't feel welcome in the first place. Some talk about helping a ghost fulfill unfinished business or resolving a conflict. Basically, helping a ghost find peace. But Mrs. Waters had a more practical solution. Show them, Cindy."

"According to Mrs. Waters, the Nuckelavee doesn't want peace or to move on. He enjoys this world and the power it yields. That puts the Nuckelavee in a different classification. He is pure evil. Mrs. Waters recommended that we'd need more than the normal exorcism or potions. We need iron, and lots of it. Iron is the Nuckelavee's Kryptonite. Pete and I will work on that side of the plan."

"We have to time it at the stroke of midnight," Ruth Ann said. "According to Mrs. Waters, the time between 11:59 p.m. and midnight is one of the in-between times when ghosts are the weakest."

"The idea is to lure the Nuckelavee out of Carl's body," Hinkle said. "Then the ravens—that's where you come in, Nate, because you and the ravens are good buds—will surround the Nuckelavee and drive him back into his grave. Or in this case, his mausoleum."

"Then we lock the iron door and flood the creek." Cindy said, with a nod. "Easy peasy."

Nate pulled his hair back from his forehead with both hands. "Have you all lost your minds? That is the big plan? Does anyone else see the difficulty? Why would the Nuckelavee want to leave Carl's body unless he had chosen his next victim?"

"Except that the Nuckelavee is burning through Carl's body," Fiona said. "It won't be long before Carl looks like the body of Coach Riley. The Nuckelavee will be desperate and that will give us the advantage."

Fiona, followed by Aaron, joined Nate and his friends. "We might have an idea. But I don't think you all will like it."

Chapter Thirty-Two

Fiona was right. Nate hated the plan, but he couldn't see any other way.

Ruth Ann perched her hands on her hips and marched toward the hovering ghosts. "That is a terrible idea. You are asking Nate to volunteer to be the Nuckelavee's host body when Carl dies."

Nate shook his head. "If we time it right, the Nuckelavee will possess my body *before* Carl dies."

Ruth Ann pressed her lips together and muttered something that sounded like a litany of swear words. "My apologies. That is so much better. No, it is definitely not. Have you lost your mind?"

"Ruth Ann—" Nate said.

She whirled at him. "I said no! You can't do this. And I don't trust Fiona. Can't you see what she's trying to do? She failed to drown you, so the next best thing is to have you volunteer to be the Nuckelavee's next victim. How does that help us? Instead of Carl being possessed, you will be. We face the same problem."

"Not quite," Aaron said, moving to Ruth Ann. "We know Carl has been possessed at least since Coach Riley was murdered. The Nuckelavee has had quite a while to take over Carl's thoughts and control him. If it enters Nate, it will not have that much time to take command. Nate will still be Nate and can help us defeat the Nuckelavee."

Ruth Ann shook her head. "No. I won't let you."

Nate turned Ruth Ann to face him. "I know it's a risk, but I have to do this."

Her eyes brimmed with unshed tears. "No, you do not. There must be another way."

"We have learned that the smaller the human host, the faster the Nuckelavee burns through it. I believe Carl's size is the reason the Nuckelavee chose him in the first place. No offense, but you and Cindy are not that big."

Hinkle stepped forward. "I'll do it."

Nate put his hand on Hinkle's shoulder, pleased that Hinkle had volunteered. This was a new side of him that Nate approved of. "Thank you, but no. this is something I must do. Plus, I'm the fastest in our group and we need speed if this plan is to work."

Ruth Ann pointed to the tallest hill in the center of the cemetery, the spot it had gotten its name from. The granite mausoleum glowed white against a steel gray sky. "You're also going to have to be half mountain goat." Her lips quivered as she blinked and swiped tears from her cheeks. She had arrived at the same conclusion he had. Nate was the logical choice.

She shook her finger at Nate. "Don't do anything reckless! But know this—I may be small, but I'm fierce, and if this Nuckelavee creature thinks I won't come after him if he hurts you or so much as harms a hair on your head, he hasn't met me."

Nate grinned. "You're worried about me."

She pulled on his shirt sleeve. "Promise me you will be careful."

"I'll be okay."

"You'd better."

Fiona drifted toward them. "It's time. The Nuckelavee approaches. We must get into place."

Chapter Thirty-Three

Under the light of the full moon, Nate swung open the cemetery's wrought iron gates. Likenesses of serpents, ravens, and snarling wolves were worked into the gate's design in the belief that the iron images would prevent the dead from following the living out of the cemetery. Those who had commissioned the likenesses had the right idea. The images frightened the living, all right. He wasn't sure if it did anything to scare the dead, however.

In one of the books he had read, iron was believed to ward off evil spirits. It worked better than first thought because it also trapped the ghosts inside the gates, and as Cindy had said, was the Nuckelavee's Kryptonite.

Nate had also read about the belief that spirits could not cross over water. Early descriptions of the mausoleum recorded that it had been surrounded by a moat like the ones surrounding castles in medieval times.

His friends had done a lot of preparation in anticipation of the Nuckelavee's appearance. He only hoped it had been enough.

He positioned himself in the center of the open space near the iron-gated entrance of the cemetery. He would take the gamble. But he stole a glance toward the shadows. On the hill, a free-standing granite mausoleum stood gleaming in the moonlight like iridescent pearls. It housed the caskets of the most prominent founding families of Pinedale. Legend speculated that the Nuckelavee had taken possession of one of the founding fathers entombed before he had been consumed by flames.

It had been presumed that the Nuckelavee had perished in the fire. Nate believed it had escaped but didn't know why it hadn't resurfaced until recently.

The plan was simple. Entice the Nuckelavee to leave Carl's body and offer his in exchange. Right before it entered his body, Nate would lure it into the mausoleum, circle around, and then lock it inside. Like Cindy said, *Easy peasy*.

One of the things he had gleaned from books was that there were as many theories on how to deal with ghosts as there were stories about them. Some people said they were benevolent, others that they were pure evil.

The theory on ghost possession seemed even more vague. No one had a definitive answer on when the possession became complete or how to rid the victim of the possession. The Catholic Church had a long history of exorcisms as a means of ridding a person of possession, but the practice harmed more people than it saved. Its methods were being reexamined and, in many cases, deemed too dangerous to continue. Which left Nate back to square one. The hope was that Carl was strong enough to fight against the Nuckelavee long enough for their plan to work.

Carl wasn't just physically strong. He had a deep-seated sense of right and wrong. He was the guy who stepped over bugs rather than stepping on them. Nate believed the reason Carl's body was burning out so fast was that the Nuckelavee was having difficulty forcing

Carl to do things he didn't want to do. If Nate could get through to Carl, there was a chance this plan would work.

Carl's new car drove into the cemetery parking lot. The door of the sports car opened, but it took a few minutes for Carl to exit. When he did, his face looked red and swollen, as though he had been baking in the sun. He was hunched over and leaned heavily on the hood of his car. Straightening, as though the effort was painful, he flipped the keys around in his hand as he strolled in Nate's direction.

The Nuckelavee had not inhabited Carl's body for more than a few days, but the results were evident. Like Coach Riley, Carl was burning up from the inside out.

Mist slithered over the ground and curled around the Nuckelavee's legs, twisting and turning like snakes. His eyes glowed, white hot. His desire for revenge against all living things was palpable.

"I'd hoped to find you here." The voice didn't sound like Carl's. It echoed through the cemetery like the roar of thunder. The Nuckelavee looked half mad, and Nate feared it might already be too late to save Carl.

The Nuckelavee held up both hands. Wind exploded from them, hitting Nate in the chest, and driving him to the ground. The blow knocked the wind out of his lungs, and a spasm of pain shot through him. Then the Nuckelavee raised his hands again. This time balls of fire shot from his hands.

Heart pounding, Nate rolled out of the way of the flames. Bushes caught fire and smoke spiraled into the air.

Nate had two goals. To try convincing Carl to fight against the power of the Nuckelavee and to lure the entity to the mausoleum. "Carl," Nate shouted, as he backed toward the center of the cemetery. "Fight the Nuckelavee."

"Foolish boy. Carl is no more."

"Friends don't give up on friends," Nate shot back.

The Nuckelavee sneered and lifted his arms, and fire shaped like flaming snakes exploded from each hand and sped toward Nate.

Nate dove behind a tree, crashing into the bushes. The flaming snakes slammed to the ground a few feet away. Branches burst into flames and birds screamed in protest as they abandoned their homes and soared into the night sky.

The sky darkened as hundreds of ravens blocked out the moon and stars and dove toward the Nuckelavee.

Nate took advantage of the distraction caused by the ravens, and he raced toward the hill. He knew the Nuckelavee would follow. There was something in the founder's mausoleum the Nuckelavee needed to complete his goal of becoming human. In all Nate's research, he'd never found out what it was the entity wanted.

The Nuckelavee's flames were deadly. Nate spared a glance over his shoulder. The bodies of dead ravens blanketed the cemetery and still they fought on. Nate shuddered at the carnage and stumbled over the remains of a stone grave marker. His heart ached for the ravens. He wanted to help them, but they had given their lives so that he could defeat the Nuckelavee, and he must not fail.

The Nuckelavee spread his arms and another wave of flames engulfed the ravens. Laughing, he emerged from the smoke and fire and moved toward Nate. "You are next."

"You will have to catch me." Nate turned and raced

up the hill.

"Slow down," the Nuckelavee hissed, each breath releasing a trail of smoke and ash. "This body fails me. I seek another and will grant you whatever you desire. Wealth. Fame…your heart's wish."

Nate slowed, turning around as he continued to edge toward the mausoleum. The Nuckelavee grew weaker—Nate could tell by the tone of his voice. "You must have tricked Carl. He would never have agreed to sell his soul." Out of the corner of his eyes he saw Aaron leading ghosts into the mausoleum. They wore clothes that spanned centuries, while Hinkle and Cindy worked to help Ruth Ann fill the trench surrounding the mausoleum with water.

The Nuckelavee laughed, coughing up ash. "You are right. Selling your soul is such an old cliché I'm surprised the offer still works after all these centuries. But it serves its purpose. While the host is wrestling with what price they would pay, they are distracted, giving me the opportunity to possess them. You are not as easily fooled. I will have to take what I want while this host still lives. If you refuse, there are other humans who will do nicely. Ruth Ann, for instance."

Nate clenched his hands at his sides. He knew the Nuckelavee was baiting him, trying to make him lose his concentration. "You cannot have Ruth Ann. You will have to go through me."

"That will not be a problem," he hissed.

The Nuckelavee marched forward up the hill. Its steps rumbled like the footfalls of a giant. The ground beneath its feet trembled, and the grass sizzled, scorching the earth. Flames shot from his hands in rapid-fire succession.

"I have a question," Nate shouted, hoping to slow down the Nuckelavee's progress and give his friends time to prepare. "I know you weren't interested in the teachers' test scores, so it must have been the legal documents in the manila envelope you wanted. Why are they so important?"

The Nuckelavee laughed, a low, heavy sound that might have come from the depths of the earth. "To prove that I own the land, of course. If I remain in human form at the time of the total lunar eclipse, I will possess the body of the true owner."

"And who would that be?"

"None of your concern." He uprooted a tombstone and hurled it in Nate's direction.

The Nuckelavee's aim was not as good as it had been before. Nate easily ducked behind a life-sized statue of an angel. The headstone crashed against the statue, slicing the angel in half.

Nate scrambled back to his feet and raced toward the mausoleum.

"You can't outrun me," the Nuckelavee shouted as a ball of flame whizzed past Nate's face, grazing his skin.

"Always could in the past," Nate shouted as he bolted over a headstone and wove around another.

The Nuckelavee was leaving a trail of fire in his wake. Bushes ignited and spread to trees that sizzled and then burst into flames. The fire spread. It jumped from one tree to the other, in rapid succession. Sparks and blackened ash curled into the night sky and obscured the moon.

Smoke choked the air, making breathing difficult.

Nate pushed up the hill, lengthening his stride as he climbed. He had a head start, but the Nuckelavee was gaining ground. Nate needed to find a way to slow the Nuckelavee down. His only chance was to reach the mausoleum before him.

He turned abruptly. "Friends forever," he shouted. "Fight back!"

The words were not random. Those words he and Carl said to each other when one or the other was feeling down. Sometimes friendship was all anyone ever had. That and the will to fight against all odds.

"Friends forever," Nate shouted again, as he backed up the hill. If he could gain Carl's attention, he might be able to distract the Nuckelavee long enough to make it to the mausoleum.

The Nuckelavee hesitated. His eyes softened to gray, then lightened again, and then again. For a brief minute, Carl's eyes changed back to normal. He lifted his gaze toward Nate in recognition.

"Sherlock. What's happening to me?" Carl managed, though the effort to speak looked difficult. The tone of his voice sounded like he had a mouthful of gravel, but the voice belonged to Carl.

Nate's eyes teared. Carl had called him "Sherlock." It was the nickname Carl had used when this nightmare had all started. Carl was fighting back, but what bothered Nate the most was Carl's face. It was blood-red. Exactly how Coach Riley had looked just moments before he died. "Carl, you're going to be okay. Remember Mrs. Waters talking about the Nuckelavee? He's possessing you. Making you do things you don't want to do. Fight back!"

The distraction worked. Nate continued backing up the hill, while the Nuckelavee stayed still, no doubt wondering why it had lost control of Carl's body.

"He wants me to kill you," Carl said.

"Don't let him." Out of the corner of his eye, Nate saw his friends duck into the shadows of the mausoleum.

Carl staggered forward. "I feel so weak."

"Remember. You're being possessed by the Nuckelavee, but you're doing great. Keep fighting him."

"I'm stronger than you are now."

Nate forced a smile. "Hey, dude, you were always stronger than me."

Carl's mouth turned up in a smile, then his eyes widened, and he convulsed. His body jerked as his head twisted from side to side. His hands pressed against the side of his head. He screamed in agony. "Help me... I'm burning up!"

"Carl! Fight! We're almost there. We've created a moat on the hill. You must make it to the water. You can swim. The Nuckelavee can't."

Carl's breathing was labored. Doubling over at the waist, Carl gasped for air and squeezed his eyes closed. Then his eyes snapped open as his eyes began to darken. "I can't hold him off any longer. Run!"

Nate turned, but the Nuckelavee's reactions were faster. He leapt into the air. Nate saw the move and rotated in midair, avoiding the Nuckelavee's grip. It let out a guttural growl as Nate dropped to his feet and sprinted up the hill.

The firestorm jumped to the cypress, oak, and cedar trees on the hill. The acrid smell of sulfur mixed with smoke clung to the air. Planted hundreds of years ago, the trees dwarfed the twelve-foot-tall wrought iron fence that surrounded the cemetery. It wouldn't be long before the inferno reduced the trees to smoldering embers.

Heat poured from the blaze, igniting everything in

its path. Drenched in sweat, Nate pressed forward.

Just a few more feet...

A hand reached out and clutched his shoulder. The burning smell of coagulated blood, burned hair, and charcoal assaulted his senses. That was how Coach Riley had smelled as he died.

The Nuckelavee tightened his grip on Nate's shoulder.

Nate had expected scorching heat, but instead a comforting warmth surged through Nate's body. His breathing slowed. He felt detached, as though he watched what was happening to his body from a great distance away. It registered that the Nuckelavee was attempting to possess his body. He should feel something—anger, regret—but all he felt was numb.

It was like when he was eight years old and had fallen down the stairs and had an out-of-body experience. He had stood at the top of the stairs, yet he saw his body at the bottom. He knew he was dead. He knew he had broken his legs and his back, but he hadn't felt sad. He hadn't felt anything. The next thing he remembered was waking up in a hospital bed in a body cast.

"You can't have him!" Ruth Ann swung an iron crowbar across the Nuckelavee's back like a sword. He roared and released his grip on Nate. She beat the Nuckelavee over the back again, and then whacked his head as Hinkle and Cindy joined the fight, armed with iron crowbars.

The Nuckelavee screamed and stumbled into the moat, and as it did, a dark gray cloud tore from Carl's body.

"Quick," Nate yelled. "It's leaving Carl's body. You

injured it, but it won't take long to recover. Once it does, it will search for another body to possess. We must act fast. We don't have much time. Pull Carl from the water before he drowns, and everyone get into position."

Chapter Thirty-Four

With Ruth Ann by his side, Nate stumbled into the mausoleum and sank down on a granite bench.

Cindy had volunteered to rush Carl to the hospital while Hinkle continued to work with Fiona and Aaron to shore up their defenses.

The walls inside the mausoleum were of white marble, with veins of gray and black running through it like the roots of a tree. The air smelled musty.

There was a stand-alone casket in the corner, as well as vaults that held the bodies of the descendants of the founding father of Pinedale. Betting that the iron theory was correct, his friends had stacked iron rods in the corner to use to fight the Nuckelavee.

Images of angels covered the walls, and gargoyles made of some kind of metal were perched on marble pillars. The half-dozen creatures sat on granite benches or in alcoves cut into the walls. The gargoyles had gaping mouths, large teeth, the head of a lion, the body of a goat, and the long tail of a snake. Five-pointed stars—or pentangles—circles, and knotwork designs were etched into the marble columns in the center of the mausoleum.

"Whoever designed this place was obsessed with demons," Ruth Ann said, breaking the silence.

"Or possessed by one. You saved my life. Again."

She joined him on the bench. "My guess is that the Nuckelavee won't come in here unless we give him permission."

He sat up, pushing to his feet. "You have your evil monsters confused. Vampires are the ones who need permission to enter. I think the Nuckelavee can go where he wants."

"You're probably right. I've been doing a lot of reading about ghosts and monsters lately. They're blending together. But I think I figured out why he was having difficulty possessing you."

"I'm not sure I understand. From my point of view, I thought the Nuckelavee was succeeding."

She shook her head. "Not really. The Nuckelavee looked frustrated while he was trying to possess you, which got me thinking about something I read. The good news, if you want to look at it that way, is that ghosts have an easier time connecting with someone who has had a near-death experience, which might explain why you can talk to Fiona so easily. But I don't think ghosts can possess someone who has had a near-death experience."

"Okay, but you were pummeling the Nuckelavee pretty hard, so I think it was more about what you were doing then me having had an out-of-body experience."

"Thank you for giving me some of the credit, but the Nuckelavee gave up. He was already loosening his hold on you when I attacked. When this is over, we'll be experts. We should start a club."

"You can be the president and I'll be your muscle."

She studied the iron rod in her hand. "Thank you."

"For volunteering to be the muscle? No, need to thank me. That's a given. If we start a club, you'd be the logical choice for president."

"Not that, silly. Thank you for not dying. I don't

know what I would do if you died."

Nate pulled her into his arms. "No one's going to die."

"Do you think Carl will make it?"

"He's a strong kid—body and soul. I must believe he will be okay."

The mausoleum shuddered.

The gargoyle on the bench toppled over and crashed on the marble floor.

Startled, Ruth Ann jumped to her feet, and then, with a sheepish grin, she settled back on the bench. "Sorry. Just nerves."

Nate put his arm around Ruth Ann's shoulders. "We're going to make this work. We won't let the Nuckelavee inside until we're ready."

Ruth Ann lifted her chin and smiled. "Thank you for not lying and saying it was just the wind." She swiped at her tears and began pacing in front of a bank of vaults. "According to the books Mrs. Waters gave us, when this mausoleum was built, the people in Pinedale feared that a malevolent spirit had followed them from Europe in the form of a raven. There is a good chance that whoever this ghost was, it traveled on the ship with Fiona and her father. These symbols were meant to keep the Nuckelavee from possessing their loved ones. The reason the air smells stale is that it was also believed that evil spirits can slip through cracks in walls. The mausoleum is airtight. If we succeed in luring it inside, it will be trapped."

Nate reached down and picked up the gargoyle that had fallen to the floor and placed it back on the bench. "Interesting. I think this thing is made of iron."

"Gargoyles are supposed to have the power to ward

off evil spirits. Whoever made them must have been expecting the Nuckelavee."

"I agree. Same plan as before," Ruth Ann said, "but with a twist."

"I'm afraid to ask. What's the twist?"

Ruth Ann handed Nate the iron rod. "I'm the bait."

Chapter Thirty-Five

"Absolutely not," Nate said.

"I just told you that the Nuckelavee won't try to possess you. He's not going to waste his time possessing animals. He needs a human host, and the only other one around is Hinkle, and Fiona and Aaron and the ghosts they raised are protecting him. I'm the only logical choice. It must be me."

"Logic took a vacation the moment we accepted the existence of ghosts and that there was a psychopathic killer who possesses people and turns them into charcoal briquets. You're not risking your life."

"Fiona and Aaron are confident the ghosts they've raised will help us." Ruth Ann said, trying to cast a positive spin on an otherwise insane situation.

"I hate this."

"Duly noted."

"Now you're sounding like a lawyer, which makes you harder to argue with. I liked it better when you said you were going to medical school."

"Maybe I'll do both. You need to get in position. You hide behind the door and wait for my signal."

"Or option B," Nate said. "If I believe you are in danger of being possessed, I will attack. Are we clear?"

"Option B sounds good too."

Nate nodded, not knowing exactly how the ghosts could help against the Nuckelavee, but he kept his mouth shut. Thinking positive was the way to go. He pressed against the wall on the side of the door, holding the iron rod in his right hand. When Ruth Ann opened the door, theoretically, the door would hide Nate from the Nuckelavee's line of sight, giving Nate the element of surprise.

Then, theoretically, Nate would use the iron rod like a sword, bash the Nuckelavee into oblivion, and drag its sorry cloud-like self into the mausoleum. Their next step seemed even more daunting. Once inside, how did you stuff a cloud into a coffin?

However, Nate had never been fond of that word "theoretically." It meant that in *theory* things would work out favorably. As in theory, the door would hide Nate and he'd get the jump on the Nuckelavee. The thought kept revolving in his thoughts. What could possibly go wrong? Possession. End of the world as they knew it. Death.

Then again, it might work. He watched Ruth Ann square her shoulders and put on a brave face. But he knew her. He knew every one of her expressions as though they were his own.

He knew that when she purchased chips from the vending machine, she had received a grade she thought she didn't deserve on an exam. When she purchased hard candy, she was cramming for a test, and when she ate a chocolate candy bar, she had a crush on a boy or had received an A in one of her classes. He was still working out that last one.

What was certain was that she was as scared as he was, yet she kept telling him that everything would be okay. It was so like her. She didn't want him to worry. But he did worry. He hated the idea that she was putting herself in danger. It should be him. He didn't care if something happened to him. He'd never told her what she meant to him. That his day only got better when he knew he'd see her in school.

"Ruth Ann? There's something I need to tell you before you open the door."

She turned toward him and smiled. "I know what you're going to say, and you can tell me when this is over." She swung the iron door open.

From his vantage point, Nate viewed the scene through the space created between the door and the door jamb. A charcoal shadow hovered in the doorway. Its form morphing into many shapes over the course of seconds, from animals to humans and then back again. Each time it changed shape its eyes glowed either ash white or blood red. When he saw the images of Coach Riley and Carl, Nate realized the shapes represented the various beings it had possessed.

In the background, Cemetery Hill was a burned-out shell, with pockets of fires dotting the landscape of ash and blackened tree stumps. In the distance he heard police and firetruck sirens, but they would be too late. He, Ruth Ann, Hinkle and the ghosts were on their own.

The Nuckelavee's cloud-like form drifted over the mausoleum's threshold. It quivered, then settled on the shape of someone dressed in clothes that reminded Nate of George Washington or Benjamin Franklin.

"About time," the Nuckelavee rasped out between breaths as he came closer to Ruth Ann. "Ah, you will do. Yes, you will do very nicely indeed." He reached out his hand toward her.

Then his eyes widened. "Noooooooo."

He raised his hand and struck Ruth Ann across the

shoulder. She sailed into the air and landed near the broken gargoyle.

Nate's anger boiled to the surface as he spun from behind the door and lunged forward.

They had miscalculated. The Nuckelavee had moved faster than light in the attack on Ruth Ann. Why had it turned on her? Was she all right? He wanted to go to her, but if he didn't contain the Nuckelavee it might attack her again.

Wielding the iron bar like a sword, he plunged it into the Nuckelavee's chest repeatedly. "Die, you miserable monster, die!"

Reaching to grip the iron rod with both hands, the Nuckelavee roared in pain and tried to pull out the iron rod. When its hands made contact with the iron, they melted from the bones as it swayed on its feet.

Hinkle, Aaron, Fiona and at least a dozen ghosts flooded into the mausoleum.

"Damn," Hinkle swore. "We didn't see it enter the mausoleum. We just heard the screams."

"Keep this monster occupied," Nate shouted as he raced over to Ruth Ann, sliding across the marble floor and dropping to kneel beside her. Nothing mattered except her. He had never been so frightened in his life. He lifted her head in his arms. "Ruth Ann? Ruth Ann!"

Her eyes blinked open. "I'm okay. We must get the Nuckelavee inside the casket while it's still vulnerable."

"On it," Aaron yelled, motioning to Fiona and the other ghosts to follow his lead and block the Nuckelavee's exit.

Nate helped Ruth Ann stand. Together they rushed over to the far corner and opened the casket.

"It's lined with iron," Nate said. "Nice touch."

"I have an idea." Hinkle grabbed the gargoyle as he might a football, while Ruth Ann reached for one of the iron rods and also tossed one to Nate.

"Time to play Destroy the Bad Guy," Hinkle arched the gargoyle over his shoulder like a football and released it in the direction of the Nuckelavee, who was fighting off the ghosts.

It sped toward its target.

The newly risen ghosts who were fighting the Nuckelavee reacted as though they were still living and dove out of its path.

The gargoyle made a direct hit and decapitated the Nuckelavee. Its head plummeted to the ground and rolled to a stop against a marble pillar.

"Awesome throw!" Nate shouted as a roar of cheers erupted.

Hinkle, grinning from ear to ear, scooped up the Nuckelavee's head and lobbed it into the coffin.

But the monster wasn't vanquished.

Nate, Ruth Ann, and Hinkle pressed the attack, driving the Nuckelavee toward the coffin. It swung aimlessly at its attackers. Each blow from the iron rods weakened it further as images of those it had possessed appeared and reappeared.

"It's time to finish this," Nate shouted. Gripping the iron rod like a sword, he swung the blade against the Nuckelavee's body. The force lifted it off its feet and it toppled into the coffin.

Together, they closed the lid over the Nuckelavee.

The sound of sirens grew louder.

"It sounds like the police have arrived," Ruth Ann said. "Do you think they'll believe us?"

"I don't believe us," Hinkle said, "and I just lopped

off the head of a really bad guy."

Nate glanced toward his friends, who all burst into laughter.

Chapter Thirty-Six

At midnight, that same evening, Nate waited for Aaron's memorial to begin, positioned in his vantage point on the football bleachers. The total lunar eclipse had lasted only minutes, and the event had come and gone without incidence. The football field was crowded with teachers and students, and soon the fireworks would begin. Everyone was in a celebratory mood.

Except Nate was restless and couldn't quite settle down just yet. He supposed it was the aftereffects of the adrenaline rush he'd felt fighting the Nuckelavee. Or that was what he told himself.

Fires smoldered on Pinedale Cemetery Hill, but Detective Morrison had told everyone that the excitement was over and congratulated Nate and his friends for defeating the Nuckelavee and solving the mystery of Aaron's death. The Nuckelavee had been secured. That's how Detective Morrison had put it. Everything was tied up in a neat bow. But hadn't Detective Morrison said once that he was suspicious when things were tied up too neatly?

Nate couldn't shake the feeling that it wasn't over. For one thing, he didn't believe Coach Riley was the only one involved in the cheating ring. Unknown was the identity of the man with the garlic-smelling breath who had helped Coach Riley kill Aaron. Most likely the Nuckelavee had killed him too.

Ruth Ann joined him on the bleachers and slipped her hand in his. "I thought I'd find you here with Edgar and Allan. They fought as well as any of us."

"Yes, they did, and I gave them field crickets as a reward."

"Eww."

Nate laughed. "Ruth Ann…"

"No, let me say this first. I know you are still worried about the Nuckelavee, and it is understandable. Even after you've run a track meet you are like this. All jumpy and agitated. Before a race you get an adrenaline rush that helps you run like the wind. But when it is over, there is a letdown and you start second guessing if you ran as well as you could have. The Nuckelavee is locked in a casket lined with iron, inside a mausoleum with round-the-clock guards. Please stop worrying and start enjoying this amazing night. You deserve it."

He put his arm around her shoulder. "We deserve it."

There was a loud boom, and an audible sigh from the crowd as an elaborate display of lights lit up the black velvet sky. Fountainlike bursts of color, in vibrant shades of purples, reds, golds, greens and blues, exploded as trailing stars of light showered down over the spellbound crowd. The students erupted in a round of applause, shouting for more, and were rewarded with another round of fireworks.

It looked as though everyone from Pinedale High School was attending Aaron's memorial. Nate had never seen anything so lovely as the fireworks.

He paused, smiling. No that wasn't true. He stole a glance toward Ruth Ann. She stood beside him, so close he could hear her breathing. She was the loveliest thing he had ever seen. He wouldn't tell her, of course. It wasn't that he thought she might tease him. It was because he was afraid she wouldn't take him seriously. Like the time he told her that he loved her.

She had answered: *I know*.

But she didn't know. She thought he loved her like a friend. There was a time when that might have been what he believed as well. When had he started to realize that she meant much more to him than just a friend?

It had happened slowly, of course, of that he was certain. It was the sort of thing that hit him when he least expected it. Like the time last spring when one of his teammates flirted with her and he punched him in the face. Nate had been suspended for three days over that incident, but it had been worth it. The guy realized he had overstepped and never flirted with Ruth Ann again. There had been other incidents, each one confirming what he knew all along.

He was in love with Ruth Ann.

He squeezed her hand gently and was ridiculously pleased when she did the same. "Are you enjoying the fireworks display?"

"Very much," she said. "I overheard you check with the doctor about Carl earlier. When we visited him at the hospital, he was doing well. Is everything okay?"

"Not only is Carl doing better, but he convinced the nurses to order him pizza. The doctor said if Carl continues to make forward progress, he will be home in a few days. He's a strong kid."

"Yes, he is," Ruth Ann said, "and I'm so grateful. But he survived because you never gave up on him."

"*We* never gave up on him."

She leaned her head against his shoulder. "The

students and teachers don't realize how close we came to disaster, do they?"

"That's for the best. Did your parents mention anything about the legal document I gave them?"

"They said it might take a while to read over, and their guess is that additional lawyers will have to weigh in. I'm curious. Who do you think the Nuckelavee meant when he said his goal was to possess the body of the true landowner of Pinedale?"

"Wish I knew. We may never know, but it's in the hands of lawyers now, and that is a good thing. I know it's late, but would you like to see a movie tonight? Mom's showing a series of Sherlock Holmes films, and I can arrange for a private showing."

He wanted to tell her how much he loved her. But the intensity of his feelings scared him, and he worried how she would react if she knew. For once in his life, he wouldn't race ahead at full speed. He would slow down and take one day at a time.

"Will there be popcorn?" she said.

"As much as you can eat."

"And chocolate? I'm in the mood for dark chocolate with sea salt and almonds. Is that silly?"

"I like silly."

She reached up on tiptoes and kissed him on the cheek. "I love the idea of a movie tonight, but only if you don't tell me the ending."

He lifted her chin, brushing a light kiss across her lips. "We will create our own ending."

A word about the author…

Pam Binder is a *New York Times* and *USA Today* Bestselling author. She is also a conference speaker and President of the Pacific Northwest Writers Association, a nonprofit writers organization dedicated to helping authors fulfill their writing goals.

Pam writes historical fiction, time travel, contemporary fiction, young adult, and fantasy.

http://pambinder.com

Thank you for purchasing
this publication of The Wild Rose Press, Inc.

For questions or more information
contact us at
info@thewildrosepress.com.

The Wild Rose Press, Inc.

www.ingramcontent.com/pod-product-compliance
Lightning Source LLC
LaVergne TN
LVHW051644220225
804326LV00036B/438